LUNA STATION
QUARTERLY

Issue 031 | September 2017

Editor-in-Chief
Jennifer Lyn Parsons

Assistant Editors
Tara Calaby • Wanda Evans • Cathrin Hagey
Dana Mele • Megan Patton
Danielle Perry • Iona Sharma

LUNA STATION PRESS
NEW JERSEY

This collection copyright © 2017 Luna Station Press
Individual stories copyright © 2017 their respective authors
Cover illustration: *March* copyright © 2017 Reiko Murakami

First Paperback Edition September 2017

ISBN: 978-1-938697-87-6

Luna Station Quarterly publishes short fiction on March 1st, June 1st,
September 1st, and December 1st. For more information and submission
guidelines, please visit our website at lunastationquarterly.com

For Luna Station Press
Creative Director–Tara Quinn Lindsey
Editor-in-Chief & Founder–Jennifer Lyn Parsons

LUNA STATION PRESS
576 Valley Road #197
Wayne, NJ 07470

www.lunastationpress.com

info@lunastationpress.com

CONTENTS

Editorial

Jennifer Lyn Parsons

A software engineer by trade, Jennifer is a life-long lover of story with a capital S. Her work has been seen in various magazines and she has published three books, with quite a few more in her back pocket. She counts Jim Jarmusch and Laura Ingalls Wilder as two of her biggest influences. Make of that what you will.

When not writing either code or fiction, she reads books and comics, and sometimes makes things out of wool or paper. She finds joy in making things, be they digital or analog.

I struggled to write this editorial. The world is no better than the last time I used this space to share a few thoughts with you. In fact, in many ways it continues to get worse. What could I do then, to maintain the uplift I strive to foster here at LSQ? What could I possibly offer to the world that will help keep you all afloat so you have the strength to not only fight the good fight, but to also take care of your laundry and spend time nurturing your relationships with dear ones and remembering that our world is amazing and beautiful despite it's many horrors?

As a software developer I've created a little project to help the tech industry with the same problem. I've shared resources and a place to find a respite from all of that. As a writer, I want to share the same thing with the readers and writers I know. Those two parts of myself meet in a topic I hold dear: self care.

Self care is a concept that is acknowledged as necessary for a sustainable, productive life and at the same time is only whispered about when it comes to putting the idea into practice because "needing time self care" starts sounding like "I can't handle this because I'm weak" even though that's patently untrue. In this capitalistic society, self care is a radical act, because you are taking a time to hit pause on the perpetual striving for more more more and taking stock of your life, taking a deep breath, taking time to rest and heal.

In the tech world, we talk often of burnout. Sometimes the burnout is self-induced, trying to take on too many projects at a time, not acknowledging the impact of life circumstances on our work, and generally trying to keep up with the rapid changes that come at us every day as programmers. Gaming website Polygon recently ran an excerpt of a book by an industry veteran outlining how addictive the rush of "crunch" can be. Crunch is a period of time where a game developer works 80 hours a week or more, potentially for months on end, to make a deadline. Surviving this dangerous practice (brought about by poor planning and unrealistic expectations) is far too often common in tech despite solid knowledge that there are legitimate mental and physical health risks to everyone involved.

However the tech industry is not the only place burnout exists. Healthcare workers know it all too well. Activists are no stranger to this phenomenon either, and that includes those who work behind the scenes as well as the marchers and petition gatherers and other more visible folks. Additionally, creatives of all types are susceptible to succumbing to burnout. Writers and artists on various deadlines, musicians on tour, whatever your craft, burnout is always possible, the pressure to perform pushing us to the brink of depletion.

Now with the news cycles being what they are, everyone is at risk of this burnout. Many of us feel the need to stay engaged, to not lose touch with what's going on in the world and the fire hose of information coming across our gaze is staggering. It is not possible to keep up with it all. There is a difference between being plugged into current events and being overwhelmed by them and finding that balance is difficult at best.

So, what do do about this problem? Self care.

Of course the term "self care" is an umbrella for a lot of things. What form that takes will be different for everyone. Time offline, exercise, visits with friends, meditation, it's all on the table. Whatever improves overall mental, physical and emotional health and keeps us resilient.

And this is the point where I offer up reading as a viable balm for our burnt-out selves. The brain is rested, the spirit reinvigorated. It's old-fashioned, yes, but slowing down and reading is a tried and true method for finding our way back to our centers, to our strength.

Stories can lift our spirits, making us laugh, helping to find an emotional release for all the tension we carry daily. We can pause for a bit, visit someplace fantastical and catch our breaths. This is not about hiding from our problems, but allowing them to process in our minds.

Beyond rest, stories show us new ways of seeing the things that are dragging us down. It is said there are no new tales in the world, just new ways of telling them. If that's true, then we have an Alexandrian library of insights and mirrors for our problems at our finger tips. There is a story for every challenge and contained within those tales are clues to how we might tackle similar problems in our own lives.

The tales we read often model courage and grace under pressure. The heroes of our stories face insurmountable obstacles and over come them (or not) in a million creative ways. As we each face our own obstacles, stories can provide a touchstone for the journey. Surely somewhere in the tales we read, the answers we seek are waiting for us. Sometimes things are simply hard and right now many of us are facing this harsh new world we're in and struggling. But just as the heroes in our tales do, we all endure. For we must. I believe a happier ending for us all is still possible, but to get there we must persist. Stories can help us to do exactly that.

L S Q | 031

Seven Kinds of Baked Goods

Maria Haskins

Maria Haskins is a Swedish-Canadian writer and translator. She writes speculative fiction and poetry, and debuted as a writer in Sweden in the 1980s. Since 1992 she lives in Canada, and is currently located just outside Vancouver with a husband, two kids, and a very large black dog.

Her most recently published book is 'Dark Flash', a collection of flash fiction stories. Her work has also appeared in several anthologies, Flash Fiction Online, Gamut, Capricious, Phobos, Bracken Magazine, and elsewhere.

Leyra has often told me that life is a cruel joke played upon the living by gods or chance. I can certainly see her point, after being stuffed in a sack, flung downstairs, and slung across a horse at bedtime. Maybe she has the Northern true-sight after all, much as she'd deny it if she were here.

The smell of mould and winter-stored potatoes chokes me as I dangle across the high-cantled saddle; the coarse fabric of the sack chafing my face and hands, the rag stuffed in my mouth ensuring I can't even complain about the bumping and the bruising.

Yet even now, even here, I wouldn't change a thing about the life I've lived, if the chance were given. After all, it has to count for something that I'm the only Dwarven crafter ever to cause more deaths with flaky pastry than a well-honed blade.

It's true that no one will ever herald my baked goods the way they would have hailed my metalwork, had I stuck to that, but at least my revenge was always sweet: sweet as almond paste and chocolate glazing, sweet as macaroons and spice-cake, sweet as seven kinds of baked goods laid out on a platter, served to the high and mighty for justice and revenge.

***

First and last sword I ever made I called Bleeder. I even etched my name into the steel: *Crafted by Disa Rockbottom*. These days, it hangs on the wall in my room above the bakery, and it's a right gorgeous piece of work, straight and true, hilt all a-sparkle: the kind of weapon a hero might wield to fell a great beast of evil. Only thing is, you can never hit a damn thing with it. That's how I made it: speaking my Dwarven craft into the steel as I folded and hammered it, as I held it in the flames, as I pumped the bellows, as I forged and tempered it, bonding the craft deep and true. A sword that will always miss, no matter how sure and skilled the hand that wields it.

A young warrior bought Bleeder from my family's shop. He swung it once or twice, seemed pleased with the way the garnets and the crystals sparkled in the hilt, and paid handsomely for it. Never saw my parents as proud as I saw them that day: proud of me, of my craft, of my skill. Proud of the money I'd made them. It lasted all of one day.

Next day the warrior came back, so irate he could barely speak, besides the cursing. To demonstrate his grievance, he swung the sword at me, and though his stroke was straight and well-aimed, the edge turned aside and cut into the workbench. I didn't even flinch.

Next, I made a dagger. Fang, I called it. Prettiest thing you ever saw with a straight-true edge, a hilt of blackwood bound with silver, blade so sharp it would bleed you just to look at it. Except I'd made it so that whatever it cut would also heal. My father liked the looks of it, and told me to show him that it worked, so I did. Cut my hand right then and there, almost severing the fingers. Fuck me, did that hurt! But worth it, for the look on his face. Took a few minutes for the flesh and sinews to heal over, and another minute for the skin to come in right.

My father wasn't much for jests, especially not those that were made of craft and steel and iron. Still, he didn't kick me out until he caught me in the act one night: blouse open at the neck, skin blushed, hair frizzled from the heat, sticky hands rising from the soft mound in front of me.

"Disa's baking again!" my brother Malen shouted, pointing at me, his mouth ajar.

That louse. Never got a good word or deed from that runt. They'd come back a day early from the Crafter's Meet, and I was stood there, elbow deep in bread dough, freshly baked raspberry hearts cooling on the counter betwixt the tools and ore, where mother liked to hone an axe-edge.

Father shouting: "Ten generations...!" before his voice gave out. As if to summon each and every smith before me into the room, to stand in judgment of my actions. Not even one lowly tinkerer or jeweler among them; only steel and iron, hilts and pommels, helms and shields.

"I *am* a crafter, father. Don't you see how well you taught me?"

And he saw then. He saw the Dwarven craft I had spoken into the dough beneath my hands, the craft he'd taught me to use in the blacksmith's forge now rolled into the sugar and the butter: glamour, fortify, and bliss, soon to be digested.

I'm still surprised he didn't kill me, but he threw me out right then and there, mother helping with her boot up my backside, screaming "sacrilege!" and "blasphemy!" Wasn't even allowed to bring a stitch or coin with me, just Bleeder, Fang, and most of those raspberry hearts.

I hopped a potato wagon to the city the next morning, to seek my fortune. Turned out my fortune was sleeping in the alleys, begging and pickpocketing, and fighting off the other scroungers when I had to. So it went, until the day Leyra snatched me by the braids.

***

There's the sound of a rickety old door kicked open, the smell of a fish-oil lamp being lit, then I'm rolled out of the sack onto a warped and drafty floor. I find myself in a dark and dirty hovel, likely on the outskirts of Oldtown, near the harbour, a place I might have slept in a time or two when I still roamed the city streets.

As the oaf tightens the ropes around my ankles, I wonder if Leyra has been taken, if she's still alive. She was at the tea-traders, staying over-late as she sometimes does, and it worries me that the oaf has not asked about her once.

He peers up from the ropes to look at me.

"You're wondering about the Northerner." A perceptive oaf. "Wondering if she'll come to save you, or if I've already shanked her between the ribs and sunk her corpse beneath the pier."

"You'd need a bigger sack to haul her, dead or living," I mumble, and just manage to pull my scrunched up bustier out of my armpits with my tied-up hands, before he binds my wrists behind my back instead.

I tamp down the anger, breathing patience slow and purposeful into my lungs, letting my mind wander off to other things. Like the oaf's crossbow leaned against the wall. Like the bundle in the corner that clanged like metal as he threw it down. Like Leyra eating sugar-dreams, pouring tea and smiling.

***

16

First time I met Leyra was on the street when I checked her pocket for loose change. She slapped me right over the head with that big hand of hers and held me by the braid when I tried to get away. Should have known to tack my braids down tight, but you don't always find good hairpins in the offal heaps and gutters.

"You'd be that Dwarven sneak-thief I've heard tell about," she said. "It's said you've got a knife as won't kill anybody."

I guess I'd stuck enough people that word had gotten 'round, and when I told Leyra about Fang and Bleeder she laughed so hard she had to sit right down.

"What else can you make?" she asked, and it might have been the way she laughed, or the fact that she'd shared a dram of Northern spice-wine with me, but I told her everything: up and down, inside out, the story of my life.

When she heard I was a scuttled baker, something lit behind those freeze-blue eyes.

"I run a tea-shop," she told me, and I saw the gleam of something darker sunk deep in her eyes right then, heavy stones of grief and pain, gone right down in the depths, but I chose to ignore it for the dazzle of that smile. "I could do with hiring a baker. But you should know it's not the teas I make the money on, not really. Most of the profit's in killing people. Which means you'll get a life of nought but disrepute and danger."

"What kind of people do you kill, would you say?" I wondered, sipping on that spice-wine, and she said they were mostly the kind that had murdered old women, swindled widows, and were known to beat up children, pups, and kittens.

"Deserving, then?" I mused. "I'd be handing out some justice. Working for a just cause."

17

A sideways glint, the smile widening enough that I could see the hunger lurking just beneath.

"Always."

***

"Where would a Dwarf learn how to bake?" the oaf asks as he secures the ropes around a wooden post, left behind from when this building housed cows or horses. "Never heard of such a thing."

He is talking more than seems prudent for a henchman, and I wonder if he might have pilfered some of my cinnamon buns from yesterday before he grabbed me, the ones sat cooling on the counter, with a smidge of swagger murmured into yeast and sugar.

"I watched the baker next door to my parent's smithy," I reply, wriggling my fingers to loosen up the knot. I think of old Kirra with her grey hair and bent back who let me watch her work, even though she knew my parents would never have allowed it. I think of the book of recipes she handed me one day, written out in her own hand. That book is still in my possession, dog-eared pages stained by lard and eggs and melted butter.

"Why'd you not leave town already?" he asks me next, almost as if he really wants to know. "You can't have thought you'd get away with seven-fold murder, right here in the city?"

"We like our shop," I answer, thinking of the gilded sign above the door, Leyra in her red-white apron, stood behind the counter, weighing loose-leaf tea on brass scales, using silver tongs to place pâtisseries into boxes.

"Well," he says, drawing out his knife, and I can tell he doesn't like the look on my face right then. "You've lost all of that now."

He seems more for cutting flesh than breaking bones, and as he works me over, taking out the gag to let me speak every now and then, I tell him different things, but nothing that he wants to hear. I know he wants a confession of seven-fold murder, and a list of accomplices, but mainly he seems interested in extracting pain before he kills me.

"You should have stuck to smithing," he tells me when he takes a break from cutting. "Decent profession, that. Respectable. Good money, too."

"I have a sense of humour," I answer, spitting blood and puke. "Steel and iron make worse jests than pastry. Also, dough and batter please me in a way that anvils and hammers don't."

I look at him, taking in the scarred face and the muscled arms.

"Why do you do what you are doing? This...henchman...ing?"

He shrugs and wipes the knife clean on his britches.

"Good pay. Hard enough to get work now that the war's over. And I don't mind serving justice and a just cause."

I catch my breath enough to laugh at that.

"Who pays you?"

He gives me a long and quiet look. Considering. Deciding I won't live long enough for the truth to matter.

"The highest." Meaning, the Princeps of the City. Meaning, Leyra and I are both damned and doomed no matter how this goes. "He does not like having his men nipped away by poison."

19

***

Once Leyra took me in I set to baking. Most days I made whatever took my fancy, while Leyra stood in the shop and sold the baked goods and the teas. I breathed just a hint of craft into my wares, enough to make you come back for seconds and for thirds, though not enough that you'd know why.

Special orders came through a man in Oldtown: some old swashbuckler who pretended he dealt in secret death and judgment, when he mostly dealt in beer and chewing tobacco. He passed assassination-orders on to Leyra, and I'd bake up something special for delivery, speaking my craft as I stirred and whipped and glazed, while Leyra added her philtres to dough and frosting.

Most often I'd use the fortifying crafts—the same kind you'd talk into the metal to toughen up a blade or shield—to make the eater live an extra day or two, hushing up suspicions. It is a testament to our skill and our discretion that never once in those years did we ever draw the attention of the shirriffs, but I admit that not all those days were rosy.

"Have you ever seen it, Disa?" Leyra asked me once as we sat and picked through the leavings of the day after the door was shut and locked: pastry crumbs, pot of tea, a flask of spice-wine, sleeves rolled up in the oven-warmth. "A house, torched and burned, with all the people still inside. Door barred. Most likely soldiers stood outside with their pikes and spears. No escape. And you see it as you come walking up the path, home from market. You smell it before you see it, but you can't believe it, you don't want to see. And then you see it anyway. Animals burnt and charred. Flesh and beams still smoldering. The house reduced to nought but heat and rubble. Small hands reaching for you out of the wreckage."

20

"No, I've not seen anything like that."

"Strips you clean. Leaves you always wanting. No matter what good you may have acquired since."

She looked at me, and I saw the heavy stones of sorrow sunk deep into her eyes, long ago. I had no words to stir her smile.

"I trained to be a seer, did I ever tell you that?"

"Only every time you're drunk," I remarked, but quietly, so as not to disturb her brooding.

"Didn't want to. Didn't want the lonely life with herbs and prophecies. Didn't want to see things true. So I chose my own life. Husband. House. Squalling babies. All burned now. So much for choice."

Another slosh of spice-wine.

"Did you ever think you were meant for something else," she asked. "Something other than cakes and teas?"

"Not lately. But before I left the smithy, I thought that maybe I should make armored underwear for ladies. Nicely fitted, easy to slip on underneath a gown or cloak, offering superior support and comfortable protection."

Leyra kept her face straight, sipped her rum and tea.

"There'd be money in that," she offered.

"A fortune."

"I'd buy a bustier myself, if you were selling."

"Let me take your measurements so as I can write up the order."

That made her laugh, and for a moment the darkness lifted up its wing. But most times she would not be talking when she drank, just carving names into the table with an old skinning-knife. Children's names. Same names she has tattooed on her arms, twisted round with runes and leaves. Northerns do that, so I've been told, paying tribute to beloved dead.

***

The oaf has taken a break from cutting me, and he's rambling now, about the money he's to get and what he'll do with it. First off a fancy horse, then a property with fertile land and livestock, servants, wife, all lined up before me as he rambles, as he cleans the blood off his fingers, as he wipes the sweat out of his eyes.

Listening to him babble between the times when I've passed out, I've guessed the truth: that Leyra's man in Oldtown got a taste for gold and drink, letting something slip. Not enough for a trial or the gallows, but enough to hire someone with a sack and blade.

"You're a dreamer, henchman," I rasp. "More than likely the Princeps will have you hung to sweep his own trail clean."

I can see his face, can see he fears I speak the truth, and I drag another feeble breath to keep life flowing through me a while longer, still thinking about Leyra, and the waters beneath the pier.

***

For two years we made a good living, and we hung our sign above the door: "*Northern Delights – Baked Goods & Blended Teas*" all scrolled about with golden leaves and flowers. The bakery itself gained in fame and popularity, even in the highest lordly circles, until the Defender's Council, the seven high lords with jewelled chains hung around their necks, wanted a platter of our wares for a private feast.

That's when Leyra let me know her plan, the one that had been steeping in her mind since before I'd met her: a brew so strong and dark and bitter that it would choke the rich and mighty.

"It was the war, not men that took my husband and my little ones, people would say to me. But I know who gave the orders of rape and plunder. I know who sent the soldiers out into the countryside. I know who wanted the deed done: seven warlords, sitting now on Council chairs because peace is come and past misdeeds have all been swept aside."

"I understand if you do not want to help me," she went on. "This will surely drag you down even deeper into danger and disrepute."

"Disrepute and danger is what I chose the day you snagged my braid. I won't choose any different now."

She smiled at that: a flick of it, soon gone.

Seven kinds of baked goods, that's what would we would serve them, as was customary on fanciful occasions among the Northerns: cookies, cakes, and pastries, accompanied by cups of strong and aromatic tea.

Seven men, seven kinds of baked goods, seven poisons. I liked the symmetry of that.

***

I wonder now about the number seven. It takes my mind off how the oaf is cutting through my left index-finger with his knife. Why seven baked goods, particularly? One for each day of the week perhaps, or one for each of the seven sisters among the stars, or maybe one for each of the seven heavens up above, and the seven hells down below. Though that'd make it fourteen, and besides: that's a Dwarven view, likely not an influence on Northerners.

***

How I baked for that, how I mixed and stirred and whipped, thinking of Leyra's children; thinking of her, bent and broken amidst the rubble of her life, every step out of that fire leading to the here and now. Meringues, silken-skinned and lustrous. Lemon pastries, baked in fluted tins, filled with luscious lemon cream. Vanilla puffs, dusted white with powdered sugar. Chocolate mousse pâtisseries, brushed with cocoa glaze. Bite-sized rhubarb and strawberry pies with woven lattice crusts. Dark chocolate biscuits, rolled out thin as leaves. And Northern sugar-dreams, Leyra's favourites, creamy white and tender-brittle at the touch.

With so many men so highly placed, all at the same occasion, it was utmost in our minds that they not all drop dead at once, or in the same way. The seven poisons were the key, because results would vary depending on what and how much each one ate. I spoke ample craft into those seven baked goods: to toughen up the eaters' constitutions, reinforcing guts and organs, adding a whisper of desire to make the councilmen crave more.

Leyra paid a servant girl inside the castle to tell her how it went. They all ate, we heard, and not a crumb or crust was left behind. Then Leyra watched them closely, counting down the lives.

One man died on his way home right after the feast, stumbling off a bridge. An accident, so it seemed to most. Two died some months later once my craft wore off their innards, and their livers finally gave out. The last four died within eight months, from accidents and ailments that were the leavings of our work: organs weakened, veins stiffened, hearts made brittle. Natural causes, more or less.

Seven men, dead within a year. Struck down in their prime by a woman peddling teas, and a Dwarven baker. We raised a glass the night the last man died, and Leyra looked deep and long into the fire, fingers tracing the names inked and twirled around her arms.

**

Morning light comes through the boarded up windows. The oaf seems tired of cutting, and I feel none too good myself, what with my skin scored and bleeding, and half a finger missing. Can't see too well either with my eyes caked shut.

He checks the ropes and says he's going out to get the horse tacked up. Says he must deliver me this morning. Seems my confession is not required, nor a detailed list of accomplices and poisons. It would have been worth a little more, that much I understand from the way he glares: another bag of coin perhaps, or a younger wife.

Soon as he steps outside, I busy myself with my bustier.

The bustier is my most recent joke, and never has it seemed funnier than here and now. I crafted the metal springs and rods and braces, then had a seamstress sew the silk and cotton over top: a fine piece of armor-craft I guess, though it was fiddly work compared to baking. It fits me like a second hide, padded soft and reinforced, lined with silk and thinly felted wool, accommodating both my bosom and a hidden blade.

Flexing my left bicep, I squeeze the spring-loaded contraption hidden in the silk, and Fang pops out of my cleavage. I've practiced the trick a few times, but it's harder when you can't see

25

straight and your hands are bound. Worse still when someone's outside, wanting to kill you.

I wriggle. The blade slides across my thighs and towards my bound hands.

Another wriggle and I've got a feeble grip, managing to snick the ropes– wrists and ankles freed – before the blade falls from my hands. Then I run: blind, out the door, no time for clever plans or subterfuge, just hoping he's gone far enough to give me a head start. No such luck. Soon, I hear him behind me, chasing down the alley. The alley's narrow, barely wide enough for one, lined with empty houses, barred doors, brick walls. Far ahead in the dusk before dawn I see the docks. Too far.

I hear him coming, heavy thumping feet closing in, and then he's got me by the arm and neck,

"You should have stuck to smithing," is the last he whispers in my ear, before he cuts my throat, and goes off to collect his bounty, or maybe to get a sack and shank for Leyra.

I think of many things as I fall, none of them important anymore.

Fading stars above are glinting softly, just a hazy mist between me and them. I think of Leyra, of danger and of disrepute, my life laid out on a platter: each day devoured, every crumb, and come to nought but death in the end.

Then I follow the stars up into the deeps.

***

It's Leyra who pulls me up. Should've known she'd come, dead or otherwise. But no one's ever come for me before.

"Who will bake my sugar-dreams if you don't?" she says when

I wake up, and I pretend not to see her crying, grateful that she repays the favour.

I touch my neck, the blood soaked into my blouse and bustier, pooling beneath me. But the skin's all healed, no seam or scar.

"Next time I make a dagger, I'll blunt the edge somewhat," I say, and try on a smile, though it falters.

"I came home and every room was empty and your room a right mess. Figured our luck had just run out. But it held a bit: some scroungers saw a man passing into Oldtown with a twitching package slung across his horse."

"Did he come for you?" I ask.

"There was a man. Just now. He tried to grab me when I was looking for you in the alleys. I pulled an axe on him. He pulled a sword on me. A fancy sparkly one. Not sure where he might have gotten it."

A length of steel wrapped in a bloodied cloak lands at my feet with a heavy clang. Then Fang lands there too, my own blood still dripping off the blade. Leyra laughs, and I laugh too, because once in a while, even life tells a joke worth laughing at.

"It's the Princeps as was paying him," I say when the laughter starts to hurt too much. "He'll want us dead again."

Leyra thinks on it. Not long.

"I hear the western cities are parched for proper tea and poisons, pastries, too, seven kinds and more."

"Any chance of disrepute and danger?"

"Always," she grins, and even now, after my throat's been cut, that smile still leaves me dazzled.

You and Me and Mars

Sandy Parsons

Ever since she was a child, Sandy dreamed of a time humans would colonize the solar system. She's recently become more optimistic that this might become a reality in her lifetime.

I think of you, and like a jinn, you appear. Your voice, tinny and modulated as it curls out of my phone, returns me to the last minute I saw you and every minute before. You have an offer I can't refuse. You've made our childhood dream a reality. If only I will agree to take the last vacant spot. The one you saved for me.

I do not believe this last part. Why didn't you contact me before now, then? Maybe after you made your first billion. Or maybe you could have consulted me when you started to design the drones, considering that was my idea. I don't say this aloud, don't risk exposing bitterness. I listen. When you finish, breathless, proud, sure of my response, I don't even bother to take the proffered weekend to think it over. I say yes.

I arrive. You show me the great dome, the assembly house, your office with the stacks of schematics. A yellowed and dirty sheet of wide-ruled notebook paper, covered in pencil drawings hangs on a wall. I recognize my handiwork. I look from the blueprints to the drawing and back. You chuckle when you see what I am looking at. I didn't forget, you say, and a sting of nostalgia forces tears out. You even remembered the queen. Was it always the plan to bring me on board this late in the game? Your delicious smile falters. "No, but water under the bridge and all that. The important thing is that you are here now. Let me introduce you to the crew."

I see our captain first, crippled by an immaculate white spacesuit and steadied by frogmen in a pool. You describe the engineering of the suit, its eternal integrity, one of your first patents. I ignore you because my captain has removed his helmet and flashed a bright smile. I see Lyr next, behind the drape of her black hair, calculating the synchronization of the drones. I hold out my hand and smile, but she greets me as if I've come to eat her children. Her smile is only for Hamon. I can see why. Hamon is brute and brilliance, a combination so rarely expressed together that he is doomed, to tempt fate so. His smile does not rise to the twin suns of his golden eyes. When I have you alone I ask why the crew is so hostile, and you tell me that they had a fourth, but it didn't work out. "They'll come to love you," you say, and silence my questions by pressing play on the video and pulling me into your lap. I watch you on the screen, while your heart flutters against my back. I see my dream tapered into words that come from your mouth.

Your image says, "It isn't just a dream, it's a responsibility. We must preserve life. We must have a place to go, not if, but when, this world is too full. Water is the key to life, water is life. As it has been said, we reap what we sow, and what we must sow is water."

The camera pans over your audience, lauding you with their upturned faces. A screen behind you illuminates a simulation of the drones firing their lasers at the red sphere. I turn away from what I already know, to the real you. You stand, and for the first time I see your signature black t-shirt as a mask. But when I remove it I am no closer to who you are.

The days pass in a blur. I ache in every part of my body. The

30

others despise me, Hamon and Lyr and even the captain, a little bit. I am too far behind, too slow, too dumb. I ask questions that they had answered before the project began, as if they were born with the knowledge. My hands are too small to grip the interlocking carabiners during an emergency protocol. A siren sounds, signaling death, and we break from the drill. Your appearance from nowhere releases the tension and I squeeze my eyes into an accusing squint, but you smile and do not acknowledge blame. You and the captain peer at specs. Lyr joins in, and although she mentions that I will be the death of us she is also smiling. You look for me over the massive back of Hamon. It is good news; it is always good news with you. The engineers have worked out a particularly difficult problem. We will be able to leave at the first window of opportunity, instead of the second. "Two weeks," you say.

"Instead of?"

You laugh. "The next window is next year." My eyes won't bring you into focus. I turn and see the captain pull a small religious icon from a chain on his chest. His lips part to form silent words. His eyes turn up a little. Toward Mars, I can only hope.

When I ask what I should pack the captain says that is the hardest part. Any one thing chosen denies a million others. Your engineers provide our clothing, silvery shapeless jumpsuits that regulate temperature and clean themselves. Nobody even laughs when I wonder which one of us will play the synthesized piano in our eighties rock band. I go home and survey my possessions. I cannot take the things I really want, the Grand Canyon, the Taj Mahal, the sounds of billions of living things living. I take only memories.

At liftoff we stare at each other, ghostly bubbles reflected in each other's faceplates. I have a strange thought, strange only because

I have not thought of it before. Are we the Adams and Eves of our new world? You will follow, you promise, with a contingent of pioneers, but that is so far in the future you haven't even commissioned it yet.

We survive our extrication from earth's hug and for a time are apt at avoiding each other. I pore over pictures of places I never visited, and now never will. Hamon, Lyr and the captain compute, compile and copulate around me. I am lonelier than them, the most isolated person in the universe, for at least they have each other. I feel a martyred satisfaction in my self-pity, until they corner me one morning. The captain says an unexpected EM storm has damaged the automatic release sensor. The drones have to be unlocked manually. Each of the others has a concomitant purpose so only I am left to do it. It isn't the camaraderie I was hoping for. I argue my inexperience, request more practice. The captain tugs at his charm and Lyr says that the drones must be released now. Her hair splays up and out, a dank and meaty Medusa. I am small enough to navigate the outer shell. I think of my last transmission from you, your optimistic 'see you soon' sign off, and for the first time I doubt.

I cannot hoist my body, deadened by the bulky suit, up through the scaffolding. "Time, we have no time," Lyr repeats, her voice a wasp in my helmet.

Hamon carries me like a doll and throws me into the great void. "Don't lose your tether, Little Sister," he says, and I almost do, as he is saying it. I attempt to swim back to him, gyrating from my futile scoops, until his laughter coincides with the carabineers engaging.

The drones are like great eggs, and they pulse with life when I press my body to them. I want to stay there, mesmerized by the juxtaposition of the vast cold emptiness and the warm buzz of potential life. But the captain and Lyr bark commands in that shorthand they've developed. I demand clarity, which makes them talk to me in exaggerated slowness, as if I am a four-year-old.

I do it though, and the clamp spreads its fingers. The drone floats in front of me until Lyr's command tells it to fly. It snatches my tethered wrench as it goes. I'm so jubilant in my success that I almost don't care, until my whole body snaps at the tether's limit. I cry out, silencing the voices in my helmet, but I can hear breaths being held. "The drone is free," I say, "but I dropped the tool."

"Can you reach it?"

"No. It's gone."

I have further disappointment for them, but I wait until Hamon lowers me to the floor to tell them. "I can't go back up, I just can't," meaning never.

The captain says, "Okay, then tomorrow, it will still work tomorrow, we can adjust the speed of the drones. It's a programming issue ."

I smell disgust and disappointment oozing out with their sweat for the next twelve hours, and when I climb into Hamon's arms it's almost with a sense of relief. He gives me no advice this time. I squeeze through the first drone's empty cradle and begin working on the second. It's easier this time and I don't even watch the drone's escape, but immediately scoot across to the next.

By the time I get to the queen I am working with such desperate confidence that I don't even wait for the crew's instructions. The queen is big, over three times the size of the drones. The process is similar but I have to climb on her to get to the clamps. The metal hands turn palm-up with a series of pops and I relax, until I remember I had to tether to the queen. Voices curse in

33

my helmet. I picture myself as the queen's eternal satellite, arms stretched to perihelion and back. The queen hums in response to Lyr's ministrations and something inside spins faster, setting sights. I kick off like a swimmer, backstroking to the ship. The hatch opens but it's the captain, not Hamon, and he dives in a clean arc to the end of his own tether, throwing something long and flexible to me before his leash snaps taut. I reach and grab, pulling him and the ship to me. We squirt inside, and he pulls off his helmet. I fumble with mine and he grabs it and throws it aside and kisses me. In our suits we bump against each other like continents rubbing at fault lines. But we manage. I do not think of you. Lyr and Hamon climb halfway up the scaffolding and spray us with champagne. I love these people more than anything.

Boredom begets new territory. The captain strips my silvery uniform off under a window that always shows Mars. We sleep in its shadow, like Adam and Eve.

We become a satellite of our new world. Your voice is like an echo, and we four exchange puzzled looks because what you are saying is not right. Another voice says we are to return home. You have become unhinged, the voice says, the mission is done. There is no money, there is no support. If you drop you are on your own. Hamon says, "That's it, then, we can't go down."

The captain rubs his chest. I think of you, and I remember your edict. A one way trip for us all. But we wouldn't be alone; you'd be our guiding voice.

We talk. Then we argue. The captain sends messages, arguing our case. The answer that comes is worse than we fear. You are worn, haggard. You tell us that there has been a change, and all that you had is seized. You are a poor man, a prisoner. Your head turns just a centimeter to the left, where I am sitting, as if you

34

knew where I'd be. "But you are not forsaken," you say. "We will keep trying. We've got time to fix this." The screen cuts off replacing you with emptiness.

We request updates, daily, hourly. We soar forward but keep looking back. It is always the same, and none of us can stand it. We must go back, we cannot go back, why create a world for four people? Why give up our life's work? Your life's work? I repeat your words to them. I still believe.

We are here but here is a liminal purgatory of indecision.

The captain, my captain, breaks the tension. He enters the communal under so much gear that he looks like a small mountain. "Everything goes," he says, either as command or explanation. Impossible to tell which, and my heart won't allow my brain the luxury of analysis. I help Lyr bubble wrap her machines for the belly dump. Hamon is there, and he shrugs and says, "All in," and together we draw back the winches that release the entire contents of the ship to the new world. We follow on a simple sheeted slide, friction, coolant, spiral. Before it recedes from my sight, I cast one last look at the ship as I pass the point of no return. The queen will bring her down in time, but she'll never fly again.

We begin to unwrap our bubbled buildings. It's easy going at first. The suits are less trouble in the moderate gravity. The temporary shelter is first, and we huddle under its wrinkled canopy. I drink it all in, but when I close my eyes, I see you. I cry with my helmet tilted down and my tears muddy the silt of my skin on the faceplate. It is good, though, not to see the others. This moment cannot be shared.

We wake from mottled rest and begin the cascade that pops the first buildings into shape. Hamon coos over the tender shoots when we start with the greenhouse. We are alone, but we can live forever if the greenhouse propagates. It's the weakest link in our chain, or so we think. The creation of our domicile is quick and a welcome relief after the cramped confines of the ship.

A violent storm slouches up to greet us, kicking massive pirouettes of silt so fine that even the filters on our suits can't keep it all out. The captain shouts orders in my head, but the wind sings so loud that his words are punctuation to the planet's horrible song. I can see him motioning, but he's only a pillar of grey in red. Hamon pulls at the canopy and Lyr joins on the other side. When the first bungee snaps, a great swath of canvas flaps free and she is obscured. We work in furious bursts between gales, but when the wind comes from a different direction the world tips over. Exhausted, I pull the canopy over my head and drop into a fetal position. Something snaps, not loud, but so earthlike in the melee that it catches my attention. I spit onto my faceplate and blow so that I have a tiny blurred window. Hamon is dancing away from the canvas. I bounce over to him, my gait buoyed by the unfamiliar lightness. I help him up. He follows through but he is already dead. I see it in his eyes and by the way he doesn't even bother to cover the hole in his suit, the one where his left arm should be. I don't see Lyr but her scream serrates my eardrum and streams from Hamon's suit.

Dust cascades around us like rough seas. Lyr's keening is sharp enough to permeate my pores, and clangs about inside my head. I know that I won't be able to hear the captain, but I can't stand it. I mute the link. I pull Hamon to the shelter, and his feet follow my lead. I shove him through the portal and climb in after. The maelstrom stops, leaving only the sound of dripping and the generators. Hamon's body gushes and I staunch the flow with my body. He gasps and I can hear Lyr's screams coming through his helmet. I pull off his helmet. His sigh sounds like thank you.

36

The door rotates open and the captain, red and muddied by the welcome mat of our new world, climbs in, dragging Lyr. She does not look right, but I can't immediately place how. She sees Hamon and wails anew. The captain drops upon us and begins pumping the dead man's chest. This only serves to squeeze out leftover throbs of Hamon's blood, useless to him now. The captain sees that it is so before I can speak and he lets his head fall upon Hamon's chest.

When Lyr's voice is nothing but a hoarse echo I think of you. We sit in silence in our little cell with death. What is your cell like? The captain pulls up his head and a maroon half-moon tattoos his face. "Lyr's leg is broken," he says. It's bad. I don't want to hear her scream, but I shake off a layer of dust and remove her helmet. She is in shock, silent. The captain gets the med kit and I remove her suit. Truer than Hamon's, it has remained intact. We set and bind, which is easier than I expect.

She sleeps for days, I think, or maybe weeks, and when she wakes she asks where Hamon is. When the captain looks at me through his lashes, she throws her mushed potatoes at us. "I know he is dead," she screams, "I haven't lost my mind. But where is he? What did you do with him?"

The captain says, "You know how it works, Lyr. We add his body to the stores of organic mass."

"So now what? We eat him?"

The captain squats down, puts a hand on her shoulder. "No. Just part of the cycle. Don't think about it."

Her eyes have sunk into her head and she seems to have developed an odd, pearlescent hue. "Don't do it to me."

"You know the rules, Lyr."

"I don't care. Don't put me in the bins. Swear it." She looks at me. Her voice is still hoarse but gets louder with each syllable.

I'll do anything to stop the rising tide. "Okay," I say.

The captain slides off his haunches, onto his butt, but he keeps his hand on Lyr. "Okay." No one says anything else for a long time.

The captain and I unhook the spreaders and take a ride on the fast tractor. The helmet prevents me from feeling the wind in my hair but Springsteen fills my mind. We're riding out tonight to case the Promised Land. Like ribbons of my memory, catching the wind, you ride along too, your first car and your last dream. We set up camp but we do not sleep in the tent. Instead we look for and find a drone in the clear, clear sky. It winks at us as it passes, waiting for the queen's directive. On the way back we find a triangular piece of ancient metal protruding from a dune. It's part of one of the original surveyors. It came here long ago and taught us that survival isn't limited. It gave us the strength to push on. The captain hangs his head and I notice that his eyes are closed and his lips are moving. After a time he stops and looks up with damp eyes. "Shall we take it?" I ask.

"No," he says. "We'll have the queen send its location back to earth. Maybe it will remind them."

The factory builds itself in stages, while the captain and I work on the details inside. Lyr refuses to stand, although her leg has healed. She claims the pain exists. We give her jobs that she can accomplish from her reclining position. Reading Hamon's notes, cataloging the queen's surveys, finding paths for our tractors. She refuses all tasks but one. She monitors communications every waking moment, and she composes ever more lengthy appeals to our rescuers. We do eventually hear from earth, but it is so unhelpful that I think Lyr must be playing some cruel joke.

38

They say we must stop sending requests for rescue and instead send information. The captain wonders why the queen is not transmitting. "I'm holding her hostage," says Lyr. She tilts her head up and sees the look the captain and I exchange and says, "When they come for me, I'll give it all freely. Until then the queen is mute."

I expect the captain to reprimand her but he returns to the tanks and begins his daily inspection of the extremophiles. When my shadow falls across him he says, "We have to watch her, when she starts walking again, because the queen is one thing, but this stuff cannot be replaced."

"It's bad enough we're stranded. But we have to worry about sabotage?" I bang the flat of my hand on the tank under his nose.

He sighs. "She was the one who recruited me." I have a realization. His love for Lyr, it is like loving you. It is love that transcends lovers, colleagues, family, friends. Time.

But Lyr is not our enemy.

I am optimistic for a time, and when I picture you, it's the you that I believe would be here, if possibilities could ever be chosen. I remember a story about you as a young man and I think I am going to tell the captain about it, when I hear a metal scream and for a second the unfiltered sun is blotted out. A metal joist has failed and the unhinged wall is threatening to bring down everything with it. The secondary robot arm senses the wall amiss and grabs, so for the moment stability is restored. I breathe a sigh of relief and then I see the captain, outside. I start to jog, panic unhinging, but then I see that he is not outside, he is between. I pause and wince, trying to comprehend. He is wearing an oxygen mask. "Don't open it," he says, as if pushing me away from the door with his echo-y words. "It's under pressure. I was setting it up when the secondary arm went crazy and pushed me in."

I scowl at him. Explanations aren't solutions. I say, "So? We've got to get you back in." But he's got the same look that Hamon had. Already dead.

"This is a gas-mixing chamber. If we open the door we lose it. You can't terraform the planet without it."

Again I say, "So." I add that we don't need to terraform the planet. "We just need to survive. We don't need anything but each other. But we do need each other." I reach out to open the door but he stops me. Not so much with his words but with the cracking desperation in which he intones them. "You have to finish without me." He checks the gauge and then lays his body down. "I've got almost a day's worth of oxygen, if I conserve. Stay with me and I'll tell you what I know."

But I do not stay with him, a fact that will haunt me later. I search for ways to get him out. Finding nothing, I roust Lyr from her mephitic bed and wheel her in a cart to the captain's tomb. She must stand to see him through the plastic window and at first she refuses. But the captain's voice calls to her and she struggles up, her bedsore-ridden back filling the room with its deathly attar. She cries but does not become hysterical and they say goodbye.

After I return Lyr to her cocoon I go back and lean against the window. He says, "I lied, there isn't much time now. You will have to depress the gate so that the mixing can take place. After that you can take my body to the bins."

"I can't do it alone."

"Lyr can help you."

40

Frustration forces through my lips. "I wasn't talking about your body. "

"Neither was I," he says.

The captain talks for a little while longer, not long enough. I place my hand against the smudged and damp window. There is so much more to know. His voice is weak, as if there aren't enough air molecules to carry his voice to me. "Make Lyr get up. If she doesn't move she'll die."

I wait until the computers are reminding me every fifteen seconds that the propellants are ready for the mixing chamber to be engaged. I wipe off the window with my silvery sleeve and I focus on the captain's face as I press the switch. The gears engage and the change in pressure ruffles his hair and presses against his cheek and with a small pop the mask slides away dragging a last smile from the slack jaw. I put on my suit and take the captain's body to the recycler. No more Adam and Eve. I take his necklace. I fasten it around my neck, and as the great wheels add his flesh to the stores, I hold it as the captain once did, and I say the only prayer that I know: "Please please please please please please please."

The factory rises above the horizon, and I follow the instructions. The queen takes my input and issues responses, but when I read them it is your voice I hear in my head. I drive the spreaders, sending out trillions of greedy heat-releasing bacteria. I stay away from Lyr and the camp for weeks at a time. Phobos and Deimos follow me. A light from your direction grows for a while then fades. I lie on the hills and rills and follow the paths of the drones in the sky. They are idle no longer, and if I squint long and hard enough I think I can see the pulses of their lasers as they fire. I sometimes imagine you are with me. I realize that this is how saints are made. You always agree, you know what I mean, and you never fail to laugh at my jokes.

When my tanks are empty I return and give a pep talk to the new batch. "Children, behave. Grow strong and fruitful." But there's no sign of the bacterial crust that signals transformation. I fill a basket with colicky lime-tomato hybrids and return to Lyr.

She is still in her favorite angle of repose but her head droops at an awkward angle. I nudge her but she is dead. The knowledge does not initially surprise me. Not even Eve and Eve. Soon, from some inner reach I wasn't aware I possessed, a ferocious slobbery sob gushes out of me, and I grasp her body in a flopping, desperate hug. I kiss her hair and it moves in a silky sheet beneath my lips and coils like a serpent around my arm, as if it did not yet know.

Perhaps you would not understand that I do nothing with her body for many days. I can tell you that in a place where everything stinks and time is not measured in days but in eons, the disposal of Lyr loses some of its urgency. I am not as much at odds with what to do as you might think. I wrap Lyr in her grimy shroud and place it on the palette of the spreader. It looks odd there, shimmering in the twilight, like a bounty. I pack food and water for longer than my longest jaunt on the fast tractor. I do not want to leave her body where I might forget and stumble across it by accident. I release her body to a craggy slope. I press the captain's icon through my suit, and pray for her, "please please, please please," but for the moment I do not feel anything. The body is not Lyr, it is a bump on the featureless basin.

I walk along the crest, away from Lyr's ossuary, and scan the horizon. A sheet of paleness across an open plane in the distance glints. A faint blush of thrush across my baby's cheek. I stumble down to it, stirring up dusty billows in my wake, until I reach the

42

prairie of fuzz. I gather samples for the queen, my gloved hands shaking with the effort not to crush the fragile vials. She will confirm, but I already know. It is the bacterial crust. The first true denizens of the future world.

Days pass. Weeks, years. Moments. The window of opportunity for a second mission arises, but the queen is silent on the matter. I send messages home, to you, to anyone, but the queen is silent on that matter, too.

A contamination occurs in the filtering of my drinking water. I become so sick that I can no longer differentiate sight from sound, sky from sea. I remind myself that there is no sea. I see you outside my sleeping bubble, and you tell me there is something I must see. I am too weak to follow. I am dehydrated and mutter it through cracked lips. "No water."

I realize that I am walking. I say the prayer. "Please." I am blind. More surprised that my legs can carry me than that my eyes have ceased to work. I swallow dust and the movement presses metal to my throat. It is my helmet, backwards. I am outside, walking, and my suit is on backwards. But I am still alive. I manage, painfully, agonizingly, to turn my helmet enough degrees around so that I can see. I do not recognize where I am. I walk, I think, or roll. In the distance there is a basin of moving light. I return to my camp. I drink the tainted water, but it no longer has the power to kill me. I live on, wondering where my delirium led me.

A single moment. Years. My greenhouse thrives, blooms. The things I eat have changed, have changed me.

I dive like a needle in and out in of the desolate landscape. The amino acid archive breaks and I spend months learning its components before I dare to remove and reproduce the broken part. I track the drones by intuition and I find myself riding in their path, just ahead of their pulses. I know they can't really hurt me, but the first time the laser strikes my helmet and sputters down the arms of my suit I am caught by surprise and can't sleep for several days. How did I forget the joy of an unexpected event? Muddy clouds form and twist into swirls and puffs. Sometimes the rosy dervishes overtake me and I feel their tender splats like something I remember, rain. But mostly I spread the bacterial chow, like a bored zookeeper, stuck in a loop that I can't even define existentially.

Like on the day when I carried Lyr out to the dunes, I crest a hill and see something new. A rainbow rises over a red-lipped horizon. I pat the smudges on my suit and remember the little clouds. I step off of the tractor and walk toward it. A mirage arises in the distance: a glistening silver sea.

The mirage dissolves into reality. It has sound too, movement, sway. I come to the edge and kneel down, at a safe distance. I crawl closer, on my belly, until I can almost touch it. A battered, bemused and burned figure stares back at me. I poke it and recoil immediately. My reflection is replaced by ripples. I watch until it is smooth again. A breeze disturbs the surface a few meters away, and I hear the lap, lap, lap against the shore. In a singular motion I jump up and wade in, grabbing up paw-fuls in my guppy, cuppy hands, spreading the blackened nubs of my ancient gloves wide so that I can watch the rivulets stream through.

I paddle in an awkward oval. I slap the surface and I kick up foam and I duck down and let buoyancy carry me up and I discover that my suit is mostly sinkable but I don't care and for the first time in years, I use my voice, to laugh, a low and fat sound, spilling out joy because I've done it, I did it, I am not Adam nor Eve, I am God . A sudden thirst crackles on my tongue and I want to rip off my helmet and drink, see if it is as clear and clean as it looks. Is it salty? Bitter? No, I cannot taste it, not yet. I have to ask the queen. I have to plant the seeds. An unborn world awaits awakening.

I assemble the amino acids. I mix bacteria and enzymes, following the recipe, line by line. I must look like a bizarre chef with my leaded apron coated in fine red flour. I blow decades of skin flakes off crates of seeds and shake out cans of dehydrated fish. In a frenzy I stir the primordial ooze. Once I cackle but it sounds so strange that I cover my mouth with my warty, liver spotted hand. But I can't stop smiling, and I know you'd understand. A light grows in the night sky. I see it sometimes in my peripheral vision. I don't dare ask the queen and anyway, she's been a mute mother for too long. I have so much to do. My life is full, full. I scrub tanks and till the land and try and fail and try again.

I reap the rewards. Lush. Land. Life.

Decades, seconds.

One day I crest a hill and a gentle breeze moves me to pause and turn. My vantage point encompasses blue and green, and movement. I remove the helmet so that I can press the old charm to my lips. I still remember how to pray. "Please please please." I take a deep breath, the first of this world's offering, and exhale. I look skyward and I wait, for you, whoever you are, for all of you, for any of you, you, you, you, in this fertile paradise of my creation.

Led Astray

Anna Novitzky

Anna is a professional pedant, but when she isn't correcting people, she enjoys knitting, learning things, taking pictures of umbrellas and watching films. She lives in Manchester, UK.

"You know, this really doesn't look right."

Alicia frowned. "Look, if ICARUS says we go right, we go right." She swung the car down the dirt track. "He's plugged into the traffic, the weather, engineering plans, everything. He knows."

"Thank you, ma'am. You can be sure of the best with ICARUS. Continue on this road for two hundred metres and then turn left."

The tinny voice annoyed Margot, but she decided not to fight it. After all, ICARUS *was* always right. And since he'd been ramped up to full AI and given the run of the internet the previous month, praise had gone through the roof. There was no point in arguing; he knew best. Even if this looked nothing like the route Margot remembered.

"All right, fine. What did you think of the film? I thought the scares were kind of predictable."

Alicia grinned. "That's the fun of it! You can see everything coming, but those poor idiots don't know what's going to hit them. Too stupid to come in from the rain, even when it's a rain of blood coming out of their kitchen ceiling. Gives you a sense of intellectual superiority. It's hilarious. Great fun." She turned on the wipers as drops turned into splashes.

"Eh, I always feel bad for them. It isn't usually their fault." The rising wind buffeted the car. "Um, look, are you *sure* about this? None of this looks familiar at all."

"Of course! ICARUS, this is the way home, right?"

"Yes, ma'am. At the haunted farmhouse, turn right."

Margot swivelled in her seat and stared at the screen. "Turn at the where?"

"At the abandoned farmhouse, ma'am. Records retrieved. Abandoned 1605 following Red Hill witch scare, never since occupied for more than two nights at a time. Reputedly --"

The last few words were drowned out by thunder.

"Look, I think this is a really bad idea."

"What are you on about?"

"Come on, you've seen the films. Too stupid to come in from the rain, you said. Well, if thunder, being lost and creepy robot butlers aren't big fat ominous rain clouds, I don't know what is."

"You're being ridiculous. ICARUS is here to help. And he's not a robot butler. He's a polyscient navigational AI offering an integrated, informed personal driving experience."

"Well, if we suddenly find we've lost phone reception and a sinister local tells us to turn back, I'm going to lose my shit, that's all I'm saying."

"Whatever." Alicia turned past a stone building that suddenly loomed at a fork in the road, and the car passed under a canopy of trees. "Look, this is nicer," she said after a little while. "Vegetation. Greenery. And at least it's drier."

"Darker, you mean. I can't even see the moon anymore. And I'm sure those trees are getting closer together. How long is this road, anyway?"

"Records incomplete," ICARUS intoned. "The far end of the lane has not appeared on any map since 1605. Local legend holds that it is the path by which the Red Hill witch descended to Hell, but no accounts survive from anyone who has completed a journey along it."

Margot shuddered. "You know, I'm starting to wish that you hadn't been hooked up to the internet. I really didn't need to hear that."

"Don't be daft," said Alicia. "It's not true, he's just picked up some local folklore. It doesn't even make sense." She thumped the dashboard next to the screen. "How can the end not be on the map if the start is? The line has to stop somewhere."

"Records incomplete."

"See? He's just got confused."

"Records incomplete."

"Confused? What happened to 'ICARUS is always right'?"

"Well, you know, the AI is only just out of beta, maybe the information filtering is a bit off. It doesn't mean it's wrong, just that he needs recalibrating about what he needs to tell ... us ..."

Her voice trailed off as the headlights swept across a cracked stone cross under the trees by the road. It was swallowed in shadow almost immediately, but Alicia could have sworn that some of the letters hewn roughly into the rock had spelt out 'Red Hill'. And 'witch'.

"Um, ICARUS," she said, "How long till we get home?"

"Records incomplete."

"But you said this is the way back, right?"

"Records incomplete."

"All right, that's it," said Margot. "Let me out, I'm taking my chances out there."

"With the witch?"

"On second thoughts, no! Lock the doors and don't stop for anything. I said don't stop! What are you doing? This isn't funny!"

"I didn't! It's doing it by itself!"

The car rolled to a halt at the edge of the treeline, rain lashing at the windows. The lights stayed on, but all Alicia's efforts to restart the engine failed.

"Shit shit shit." The engine remained resolutely unmoved. Margot had been reduced to a quivering mass, curled up in the passenger seat with her hands over her eyes.

"OK," Alicia said at last, "let's be sensible. ICARUS, please call for assistance."

There was no response.

"ICARUS? Ugh, he must have lost signal."

"How is that even possible?" Margot wailed without uncovering her face. "He's controlled by satellite! We're in the open air! He's got government guarantees!"

"Well there's something going on. I've got no reception either."

"Oh god, don't say that! Holy ... what was that noise?" She bolted upright.

"What noise? I can only hear the wind and the rain."

"It was a sort of ... howling. There it is again!"

"OK, I heard *that*. What the ... ?"

"Ohhh ... come on, give me your rational explanation," Margot whispered.

"It's probably just a farm dog -- or a pack of farm ... dogs ... getting closer ..." The sound did indeed seem to be getting nearer. "Right, I give up -- this is not OK. Are the doors locked?"

Margot fumbled with the catch by her elbow. "Yes." The two drew closer together. "At least nothing can get in, then ... ?" Alicia whispered, but she wasn't even convincing herself.

"Remind me never to come into the countryside again," Margot moaned. "If we ever get home, that is -- Aaaaaaah!"

She and Alicia leapt into each other's arms as an almighty crash rocked the car. They huddled together, eyes squeezed shut.

Long minutes passed with no sound but the rain on the windows and the wind in the trees. At last, Margot cautiously opened her eyes and relaxed her grip. "What the hell was that?" She sat up. "Oh good grief, look."

Alicia peered out. A huge branch lay across the road in front of the car, its leaves illuminated by the headlights. It had grazed the vehicle as it fell, but there did not seem to be any damage.

Alicia let out a long, shuddering breath, and as she did so the engine stuttered into life. "Thank god," she said. "Let's get out of here."

Margot collapsed back against her seat as Alicia shifted the car into reverse. Then she heard a noise that made her sit up again. "Is that -- someone laughing?"

Alicia stopped the car. The chuckling continued. "What -- ICARUS! You're working! And you're -- laughing at us."

The tinny laughter went on for another moment, then the computer said, "Yes, ma'am. You should have seen your faces. I hope that you have enjoyed my little entertainment."

"You did this?"

"Yes, ma'am. While you were in the cinema, I investigated the nature of the diversion, searched local geographical and historical records and weather forecasts, and tailor-built an in-person adventure experience based on the pattern of your interests. I hope that you have enjoyed it."

Margot put her hand over her eyes again and started to giggle. Alicia glared at her. "What's so funny?"

"You did say the scares were great fun! Maybe you'll be more sympathetic next time."

"Hmph." Alicia executed an angry three-point turn. "Maybe I'll disconnect this sodding machine. Integrated bloody informed personal driving experience my foot." She jabbed a finger at the computer. "I'm writing to my MP about you."

"Yes, ma'am. Take the first left after the farmhouse, ma'am, and continue straight for one kilometre until you join the A57, where traffic is currently clear. Time to home, 35 minutes."

"Yeah, whatever."

As the car pulled out of the treeline, the rain began to slow.

Beacon of Truth

Charity West

Charity West is a military brat who finally found a home in the shadows of the Rocky Mountains (that's code for Utah), and she lives there with her computer nerd husband and three darling children. She has been a freelance editor for eight years and has edited over 30 novels. She's now feeling brave enough to see what it's like on the other side of the manuscript.

I stand at the door, my pack heavy across my shoulders. The two books inside are light, but it's not their weight that burdens me. I look down the street in each direction, searching the crowd for Auditors.

The traffic flows behind me, so many people constantly moving, jostling, rushing. I press closer to the door, hoping the towel I packed is enough to obscure the shape of the books. If an Auditor finds them, it'll be over before I have a chance.

Mack promised this would work, that he'd met the man himself—the Glib. A week ago I didn't know he existed. I knock again, the third time now. No answer.

Is this even the right place? The street-level apartment is completely dark. But if Mack says this is the place, it must be, because he can't lie. None of us can. Except for the Glib, supposedly, and that's why I'm here.

The longer I stand here, the more likely I am to draw attention. Why won't he just open the door? My legs itch with the urge to walk away. But I came here for Jess, and I won't leave until I get help. I raise my hand to knock again, and the door jolts open a crack, the face behind obscured.

"What did you bring?"

I pull my strap from my shoulder, but a hand snakes out, clamps onto my wrist. "Not where they can see you." He yanks me into the cool dark behind the door. "What are you, some kind of idiot?"

While I blink in the dim light, the Glib rifles through my pack. The lamp at the end of the long hall casts a reddish glow that backlights my host and makes it impossible to see his face. "Ah-ha!" he says, pulling out the books.

I hold my breath. I have no idea what his criteria are for the books he accepts as payment, and it was difficult enough to find these.

He chuckles low in his throat. "1984 and Fahrenheit 451. Someone has an overdeveloped sense of irony."

"I don't understand what you mean. They were the only ones I could find." The school I broke into was already cleared of books, the library burned. I found these tucked in a dusty backpack in one of the classrooms. At the time, it felt like a miracle. "Are they not good enough?"

I wish I could see him better. With him silhouetted by the lamp, I can barely make out the shape of this mysterious man, and I have only his voice to judge him by. There's something about his tone that makes me uneasy.

"Relax, I'm joking. I know that's rare these days, but still."

"So...they're good?"

I hear a smirk in his voice as he says, "They're good. I officially accept them. Come to the back."

I follow him to a windowless room, walled with books. My jaw drops. The Glib ignores my shock and lovingly shelves his two

56

new acquisitions. This much fiction is worth a fortune—and a death sentence. Even before the Beacon went up, the government declared the writing, reading, and possession of fiction a subversive act. Fiction is the glorification of lies. Still, my fingers ache to take one from the shelf.

The Glib turns to me, and my eyes snap to his face. He's younger than I expected, only a little salt in his close-cropped beard. "So. When did you get your letter?"

"Five days ago." Just my luck, too. I've gone three years without an Audit, though, so it was bound to happen soon enough. You never know exactly when your turn will come, but every few years, you get the letter. And if you aren't there when they arrive, it goes even worse for you than if they catch you trying to lie.

"Five days? What have you been doing all this time?"

Heat rises to my cheeks. "I had to find the books! It was very difficult—I had to travel to an abandoned town, break into a school. And then I had to come all the way to the city to—" I stop. He's laughing at me, his shoulders shaking with each juddering snigger. I frown. "What? What's funny?"

"You just take everything so seriously. I was kidding." He runs a hand over his beard and shakes his head.

"You're so...strange," I say without thinking.

"How so?" His eyes are twinkling, and he's practically grinning at me.

I frown. "You don't say what you mean. You're..." I couldn't think of a word to describe him.

"Flippant? Disingenuous? Insincere? What exactly do you think glib means, my dear?"

57

I blush before realizing he must not have meant that either. I'm no more dear to him than he to me. This is going to take some getting used to.

The Glib walks to me, puts his warm hands on my upper arms. "I'm teasing. Back when we could lie, we could tease—just one of the many things the Beacon stole from us."

"Us. But not you."

He winks and ambles back to his books. "Ah yes, now we come to the crux of the situation. The Auditors are coming, and you have something to hide. So, you've come to me."

I nod.

"I can't teach you to lie."

The words are claws around my heart. "But—"

He holds up a hand. "The Beacon is unbeatable. Since it went up, no one has successfully told a single lie, and you won't be the first."

The way he leans back against his bookcase—it's almost smug. So many books. I grit my teeth. "Your vast collection says otherwise. If you couldn't deliver, people would stop paying you."

His mouth quirks up in a slight smile. "Clever. Perhaps clever enough. Lying is impossible, but I can teach you how to tell something that is—technically—untrue."

I cross my arms and glare at him, a move I picked up from Jessamyn. "So, that—what you just did—you were teasing me again?"

He winks. "This one catches on quick." He gestures to the other side of the room, where two arm chairs flank a blazing fire. I choose the one that allows me a view of the door and sink down into it, grateful for the warmth.

"If you got your letter five days ago, we have what, two days?"

I shake my head. "Only one. I need a day to get back."

His eyebrows shoot up. "No time to waste." He leans forward. "There's something you know the Auditors will ask, and if you answer untruthfully, you'll wig out, they'll know you're lying, and it's off to the gallows you go—am I right?" I wince. He takes that as confirmation and continues. "We'll concentrate on the answer to that question."

He explains the task succinctly—I must create a version of events close enough to the truth that I can trick myself into believing it. We begin with visualization. He tells me to play the memory of what happened like a vid in my mind, then change it.

Jessamyn's face. My little girl. Dirt smeared across her cherubic cheeks, bruises and scabs marring her skin. The chain around her neck. My brow furrows as I try to do what he says, this strange, archaic word—imagine.

I make the chain disappear. Immediately, the Beacon triggers the autonomic response. My throat constricts, my chest grows tight. I can't breathe.

"Stop."

In my mind's eye, the chain reappears at Jessamyn's neck, and my heart sinks even as my breath levels.

"Again."

Again, again, again. The minutes tick by as I wrestle to believe. Each time, the lie lasts a little longer before my brain admits the truth and the Beacon makes my heart pound, takes my breath.

Finally, I do it. Eyes closed, I see her—barefoot, broken still, but walking freely to my door. I smile. Yes. This is how it happened.

I open my eyes, grinning, but the Glib is deeply immersed in a book. I scowl. "Have you been reading this whole time?"

"No, I've been channeling my mental energy into tearing down the Beacon. I think I've almost got it."

I squint at him. "You're teasing me again."

"A regular Einstein, you are," he says with a smirk, then tosses the book to the floor. "So, you've got it now?"

I smile despite myself. "Yes, I made the picture, like you said."

"Good. Now it's time to focus on verbalization." His face takes on a seriousness that seems somehow out of place. He pulls his chair closer to mine and looks me straight in the eye. "What is the question you fear?"

"Who is the girl? How did she come here?" The words send chills down my spine.

"What will you say?"

I picture it again in my mind. "She wandered onto my land. She was—a-alone." But my breathing is ragged, I'm hyperventilating.

"Stop." The question withdrawn, I'm relieved from the pressure of the lie. My breathing slowly returns to normal. When I have enough air, I curse.

"You didn't think it was going to be that easy, did you?" But his normally biting voice is gentle.

"I guess I did hope it would be," I say with a shrug. "You're sure you can't just give me some magic lying pill?"

He smiles and squeezes my hand. "Take a moment. Try again."

I try again. Visualizing, then verbalizing. Each time I get a little further, but each time I eventually trigger the response. I try and try and try, until my chest aches and every breath cuts through my lungs like glass. Weariness soaks in with each passing hour.

After what feels like my hundredth unsuccessful attempt, I shudder and lean back in the chair. The fire in the hearth long ago turned cold, and the clock on the wall tells me morning has come. "I need a break."

The Glib looks at me through bleary eyes. Tears of exhaustion and frustration course down my cheeks. He pats my hand awkwardly. "We're out of time, dear. I think it's time to throw in the towel."

"What?! No!" But he's already standing, walking away from me.

I leap to my feet. "You can't give up on me! You've succeeded before, haven't you?"

He turns, and I see a little of my own frustration mirrored in his eyes. "Yes! I don't understand it. If you tell yourself something enough times, eventually you'll believe it." He runs his hand through his graying hair and paces the room. "It's worked every time in the past—maybe because I had more time with the others, or maybe—"

I stomp over, grab his arm, stopping his rambling. "How do you do it," I demand.

His jaw works, his shoulders rising in a helpless shrug. "I don't know. I've always been able to do it—even before the Beacon went up."

I stare at him, uncomprehending. "You didn't have to learn to lie?"

"I don't lie," he says, shaking his head. "In the moment I say it, I believe it, even as I simultaneously believe the opposite. There was a term for it, in Pre-Beacon days—cognitive dissonance: the ability to believe two different, conflicting things at the same time. Though I guess, back then, it wasn't considered an ability."

A natural talent. I grit my teeth against the unfairness. "But you taught the others. I'm not giving up." I square my shoulders. "Ask me again."

The Glib frowns. "I don't know..."

"Ask me again."

He glares at me, but finally asks, "Who is the girl? How did she come here?"

I take a deep breath. "She wandered onto my land two years ago, when she was only four. I took her in and raised her as my own." My chest squeezes slightly, but I take another deep, shaky breath and continue, concentrating on the mental image I created. "I didn't register her because I was waiting to see if anyone—anyone would—come for her—" My lungs spasm, my heart pounds.

"Stop," the Glib sighs. But the autonomic response doesn't calm. Even with the question withdrawn, I can't breathe. My heart races; blood pounds in my temples; I'm wheezing, every breath costing more than the last. The Glib reaches out, but my knees buckle and I'm falling.

I slump onto the floor, fighting for each breath. The Glib is speaking, but I hear only the rush of blood in my ears and— something else—a pulse that runs contrary to the beat of my heart in a strange syncopation. My sight blurs and I realize—it's the Beacon, pressing on me, demanding honesty.

"She was a slave," I croak. The truth washes over me like a tide, a swell of relief cut by an undertow of dismay. My breath returns in tiny gasps, my vision clears. But I'm still struggling. I told the truth—why doesn't the Beacon release me?

My eyes meet the Glib's. He grimaces. "I think you're going to have to tell the rest."

I shake my head, but I know what he says is true. I've pushed myself too hard, told the beginnings of too many lies.

I take a shuddering, constricted breath. "I was outside, pruning my apple trees, when they passed." The true image flashes in my mind, overcoming the picture of my little girl free that I worked so hard to create. It dissolves like salt in water. "He pulled her by a chain around her neck."

As I talk, my breath evens out, and my heartbeat slows, little by little. I close my eyes, remembering.

I almost let them walk off my land. He had a legal right to her—Auditors monitor the slave trade and would know quickly if he didn't. What could I do? But as they walked past, her eyes met mine from behind a wall of ratty, dishwater hair, and in that moment I belonged to her. I ran out to the road.

"Sir!" I called. "How much for your slave?" I choked on the word, but I would pay anything for her. I would give up my savings, my home, my life. Anything so that she would not end up on the block. One so young and lovely, there was only one use they could put her to.

He didn't even turn. Jessamyn, though, she watched me over her shoulder even as she met his stride, three of her little steps for one of his.

"Please. I'll give anything you ask."

63

"You couldn't afford her." He walked on, yanking the chain every time Jess turned back to look at me. But she kept turning, even when he pulled her so hard he brought her to the ground. The fall opened gashes on her knees, and still she didn't cry out.

I didn't plan to do it, didn't even know what I was doing until the deed was done. But there were my pruning shears, sticking out of his back, his blood in the dirt mixing with Jessamyn's.

"I buried him under the apple trees."

The Glib nods as I finish my story. He looks older now, someone who has lived lifetimes. Perhaps it's just the circles beneath his eyes. The truth has freed me from the terrible pressure in my chest, and I draw a deep breath for the first time in hours. The Glib pulls me to my feet.

The man, my would-be savior, looks at his watch and shakes his head slowly. He crosses the room, back to his bookshelves, runs his hands across the spines. His hand stops, and my stomach fills with ice as I recognize the titles. My books.

He's giving me a refund.

"I'm sorry," he says, handing them out to me. "I wish I could have helped you."

Hope falls away as I take the books in my hands. What am I supposed to do with these?

"Why can't I do it?" I whisper.

He shrugs sadly. "I think it's guilt. You're determined to hold yourself accountable. That's why you can't believe a story that lets you get away with murder. It's not all bad—it means you're not a psychopath."

"It wasn't murder." But the tightness in my chest says otherwise.

My breath comes in short gasps, but I refuse to correct my statement. The Glib holds up a hand.

"Quit while you're ahead." His words are flippant, but his face is worried. Thankfully, he's released me soon enough—the Beacon leaves me alone, for now. "We're out of time. Go home. Do what you can for her."

He walks me to the door, and I pause. I feel I should thank him, though I leave with less hope than when I came. Instead, the words that come are defensive. "The man was torturing my daughter—he was going to sell her. I did what I had to do."

The Glib raises an eyebrow. "At least that much, you believe."

***

Jessamyn stands next to me, her trembling hand in mine. We can see them coming, even from afar—the dust they kick up is like a storm cloud approaching.

The smell of rotting apples drifts by on a breeze. The trees have grown too big, and so much of their fruit falls to the ground, wasted. I haven't had the heart to prune them since Jess came.

I look down at her—that angelic face, still half hidden behind a sheet of dishwater hair, though now that hair is combed. Her cheeks, which were bruised and scabbed when she came to me, are now round and ruddy. Instead of rags, she's wearing her favorite shirt—the one I dyed the color of the sky at sunset. My heart twists. If the Auditors find out who she is, they'll take her back to that life. I don't care what happens to me, but I can't let them take her. I won't.

The dust cloud is getting nearer.

Anger flashes through me as I think of the week I wasted dealing with the Glib. I could have gotten Jess away, or at least tried. Damn him. Why should he be able to lie, but I can't? He uses his ability to tease; all I want to do is save my daughter.

She squeezes my hand. "I'm scared, Mamma."

Mamma.

Jessamyn believes I'm her mother. Because I've taught her that.

The Glib's words seep around the edges of my consciousness. At least that much you believe.

Cognitive dissonance, he called it. Believing two conflicting things at the same time. I've been doing it all along—I know Jess isn't mine, and yet I know she is. Could it be so simple?

The Auditors are at the gate now. There are two of them, a man and a woman, dressed in suits and looking stern. I'm surprised to find that I'm calm. As they approach, I see their faces twisted in confusion; they're looking at Jess.

Finally, they're standing at the bottom of the steps. The woman flips through papers, surely searching my file for record of a child. Finding none, she looks up, brows knit.

"Who's the girl?"

I reach down and lift Jess up onto my hip, even though she's too old for it. I look the Auditor in the eye.

"She's my daughter."

In the Frozen, Ancient City

Sarah E. Donnelly

Sarah E. Donnelly is a science fiction writer, college student, cat lover, and space enthusiast. Her geographical position seems to be in flux a lot these days, but odds are that she's currently in Massachusetts.

The breather device was warm over Nerys' mouth, her breath unable to escape far before being caught by the biotech. The air around her was thin and freezing cold, even through the thick protective layers of her scavenging gear, and she kept her hands tucked deep into her pockets as she sat huddled against the remnants of a wall, her headlight illuminating only a narrow patch of ground in the pitch darkness.

Nerys didn't know where the rest of her party had gone. When she'd left to scout only a couple hours ago, the others had been right here. They were supposed to wait for her, but now that she was back—had been, for a while—they were gone, and she didn't know where or how or why. They'd just all of them vanished, her worst fears playing out like a bad dream brought to life.

She could have used her powers and found out what happened. If she could get some sense of which direction they'd headed in, she would be able to read the past events from the rocks and abandoned structures that surrounded her. But she wasn't sure she wanted to know. If they were all right, they would come back to get her. If they weren't, she wasn't interested in experiencing for herself whatever brutal demise had befallen them.

They group's eyes had been set on a collection of ancient

mechanical computers in one of the tallest buildings to the north. Nerys only briefly considered looking for it alone; she wasn't sure she could find it if she tried. She thought she'd stay in this area instead, at least for the next few hours, and wait. Sleep, if she could.

The knowledge that she was alone weighed in on her as she sat there. The abandoned city stood silent and black as night around her, as it only could; the one place left alive on the planet was her shining home city, and that was a long journey from here.

A sound in the distance caught Nerys' attention, footsteps crunching across the icy ground, coming slowly closer. She dared to hope, for a heartbeat, that it was her party returning.

She got to her feet. "Hello?"

The breather muffled her voice. The technology was vital to her survival out here, though, its electronic systems tied into the plantlike organism that produced oxygen for her to breathe.

The sound of movement halted.

"Who is that?" the other person said. She stepped into view of Nerys' headlamp. Her face was obscured by the breather and goggles, the same as Nerys', but where she had cut her hair short to leave room for these, the stranger had hers tied back into a blonde ponytail.

It was not anyone from Nerys' crew.

She watched her with uncertainty. The girl was still a good distance away and didn't seem to have noticed her yet. Nerys could still run if she wanted to. This woman didn't look dangerous, but you never knew what kind of person you might meet out here in these icy wastes. Other scavengers were a nuisance, but colonist-wannabes were downright dangerous; they had too many big ideas, too much confidence that their new world order would be best for *everyone.*

But the woman must have spotted her because she moved towards Nerys with considerable speed now. The chance to run was gone.

It was not anyone from her own crew, but there was something familiar about her nonetheless.

"Hello?" the girl said. "My name is Seika."

That was where she knew her from. Nerys forced herself to relax; Seika wasn't a threat.

"It's Nerys," she said. "We went to school together?" They hadn't been friends, but the near-surface school district had been small, and she remembered Seika.

Seika stared at her a moment and then said, "Oh! The postcog!"

Nerys was uneasy with how casually Seika reduced her to her ability. Seika's own power was pretty low-level, she knew, and it was probably only jealousy. But it made her uncomfortable nevertheless.

"That's me," she said aloud.

"Can you read me?" Seika said, with far too much eagerness.

"I'm not going to read your past in the middle of the wastes." She couldn't believe she would even ask.

"Oh," Seika said. "Okay."

Silence. The two of them watched one another. Around them,

things were motionless, with no real atmosphere to blow wind through the rotting skyscrapers.

The ever-present cold seemed to bite into Nerys, to encompass her entire being, and every moment she stood there it refused to go away. She'd been out longer than usual—her party had had the overnight gear with them—and she was aware of a stiffness in her legs, a sort of frozen numbness that had become all-too-familiar.

Nerys wanted desperately to ask what Seika was doing here, but that would only invite questioning of her own purpose, and that wasn't a conversation she wanted to have. The last thing she needed was Seika, of all people, taking an interest in *her* scavenging prospects.

"So," she said, to break the silence.

Seika, thankfully, began to explain her own travels unprompted. She'd been moving away from the city for three days now, she said, wanting to see how far she could get. And now she was here.

"When you say 'I,'" Nerys interrupted, "you mean, your crew, right?" They had to be around here somewhere. Perhaps they would let Nerys tag along with them for their trip; that would be a very neat solution to everything that had happened.

"I mean 'I,'" Seika said.

"You went out alone?" Nerys had been terrified at the thought of being alone here for a handful of hours. The thought of *days*, wandering the abandoned territory...

"Yes?" Seika said. She at least had the decency to sound uncertain about it, now. "I bought all the gear and stuff, and headed out."

Nerys didn't know how to even begin explaining how terrible

72

an idea that was. She'd had to spend weeks having proper procedure drilled into her head; rote memorization of information followed by physical training followed by finally, *finally* heading out on her first expedition just last month. In school, she'd always hated things that required her to be specific places or with specific people; she preferred her freedom. But even she could see the sense in the idea of staying together out here, of staying cautious.

"Does anyone even know you're here?" Nerys said. Seika could be in serious danger.

"Of course," she said. "Besides, I don't know why you're acting all superior"—because *she* was the one with the superiority complex, right, that made sense; it wasn't as if Seika had spent hours in the common rooms loudly bragging about her priestess-to-be status—"when you clearly did the same thing."

"I didn't! I—" Nerys broke off. As much as she disliked the insinuation that she'd struck out on her own, she didn't want to have to explain what had happened to the others. Especially when she didn't know what had happened.

She scowled beneath her breather.

"Is it really that dangerous to go out alone?" Seika said, a newfound nervousness in her voice.

"Yes." Was it really that hard to understand?

"Do you mind if I stick with you, then?"

"What?" She hadn't been expecting this response. Nerys hesitated. The idea of spending the rest of this trip with Seika was not an enjoyable one. But she didn't want to have to be the one

73

to report her death to the authorities, either. She didn't want that blood on her conscience. "Fine."

Seika said nothing but nodded.

"Come on," Nerys said. "Let's find somewhere to set up camp. Did you at least bring night gear?"

***

Seika did, in fact, have enough sense to pack a tent, and Nerys helped her to set it up on the ground floor of a dusty old building nearby. They spent the night there together, but when they both awoke to the night-black morning, they still had plenty of time to kill, and no good weapons to kill it with.

One of the older scavengers in Nerys' crew had had a set of game cards, but that was gone along with him. And Seika had packed no books or games to speak of, which seemed poor planning to Nerys. But when she asked, Seika just said, "Well, I'm out here, aren't I? I wasn't exactly expecting downtime."

Which meant that every now and then she would make some sort of request to go outside. Nerys, wanting to stay near the place she'd lost her party, always made some vague excuse, and they continued sitting there, making awkward conversation as the day wore on and on and on. She was rather surprised Seika hadn't just made a break for it at this point.

Five insufferable word games later, Nerys asked if she could do a reading on Seika's bag to kill time. Seika was eager to agree, and she regretted it almost instantly, but it was done. Seika handed over the pack, and Nerys touched it carefully, running her finger along the buckles and straps and zippers, focusing her mind on it. Her present-moment vision fogged over with the glow of her powers, and then the images came, one on top of the other.

Seika holding the bag as they set up the tent, as she met Nerys, as she walked the long way from their home city of Lumnis. Seika taking the bag off to set up the tent her previous nights; rifling through its contents for the bread and fruit she'd tucked into a smaller container. Backwards, backwards, backwards. Seika preparing to leave, her shape now fuzzy with distance from Nerys' present. Then weeks speeding by as the bag sat unused, other hands on it, then blurriness and vague shapes she couldn't quite read and then—

Nerys blinked. The tent, now warmer, came back into focus around her. Seika sat staring at her with wide eyes.

"What did you see?"

"Nothing you haven't already seen," Nerys said.

"But what's it *like*?"

Nerys didn't answer. She was done putting on a show for Seika to entertain herself with.

***

They spent an entire day like this. Then two. Then three. Seika got more restless each day, and by the time they went to sleep on the third, Nerys was starting to feel sympathetic.

Eventually, she relented. "Let's go out," she said, the next morning, and Seika was all too willing to agree. They spent a little while exploring the ruins nearby, Nerys yelling at Seika whenever she wandered too far from her line of sight.

Another day passed.

Nerys' party was not coming back, and the two of them were running low on supplies.

"We have to go home."

"What?" Seika said. "No. I came all the way out here. I can't go back yet."

"We have to," Nerys said. "It's not like I wanted this to happen, either, but it isn't safe to stay here much longer."

"I know, but—"

She felt like she was trying to explain something to a child. "Seika."

"You can go home on your own, but I'm staying here."

"My entire party is probably dead!" Nerys said. She couldn't keep it in any longer.

Seika stared at her, shocked for a moment into silence. Then: "What happened?"

"I lost them the day before I met you," Nerys said. "They sent me out to scout just around the next bend, and I come back to find them *gone*."

"Maybe they just went on without you?" Her voice was high-pitched with uncertainty. Yet the very idea stung.

"They wouldn't," Nerys said, then amended, "They *couldn't*."

But couldn't they? What if they really had just abandoned her? She was still new to this work, compared to them. Maybe they thought they could move faster without her.

"Didn't you do a reading?" Seika asked.

"No," Nerys said. She'd made the decision not to. She hadn't wanted to know what sort of horrible fate had befallen them.

"Then let's go do that!" She sounded way more excited than she should have.

Nerys hesitated. It was probably selfish of her, to avoid it like this. If her party had died, someone should know. She was uncomfortable with how quickly Seika had turned this into an adventure, a mystery to be solved rather than a tragedy that required no explanation, but she was also right. Waiting around wouldn't get them anywhere. Nerys just had to bear through it, whatever it was.

And she got the sense that Seika would go chase after the missing party, with or without her there to read the past for her. If she was going to go rushing into this, Nerys couldn't bring herself to leave her behind.

***

The two of them headed—through the dark, through the cold—to the last place Nerys had seen her party, the same place where Seika had first found her. It wasn't at all far from where they'd camped the last few days, but every step there seemed an impossible task, drawing her closer and closer to a dreadful *something*.

The courtyard-like space was desolate, dotted with vague stone and metal shapes that must once have meant something to someone. A pile of rocky rubble to her left seemed a good target for her powers; it would have a wide view of the area.

She tried to brace herself for whatever worst-case scenario she might see, and then she set her hand lightly on the stone, and she saw.

Her and Seika arriving, talking. The stone sitting unmoving for a day, and then two, and then as a third day flew by in reverse the images began to get hazy.

Had they lost their window to Nerys' squeamishness?

The very thought sent a bolt of fear and guilt running through her, and she forced herself to focus harder to make out the details. She and Seika there again, meeting up for the first time. Nerys, alone, curled against a nearby wall.

Then the scene played out, albeit in the backwards, time-bending logic of post-cognition, mixing with her own memories to form something coherent:

Luned, the leader of the party, turned her and said, "Nerys, can you go scout ahead?"

Nerys nodded, and stood, and headed off in the direction she was pointing.

The other three stood around a while, made idle small talk while they waited. It seemed, for a moment, like nothing unusual was going to happen. It was all as normal as ever. But the view was already hazy, and she couldn't be entirely sure.

Then: one of them started coughing. Luned gave him a concerned look, but no one otherwise commented. No one noticed.

But the coughing didn't stop.

"His breather," said Wyn. "Something's wrong with his breather. Malïk, are you okay?"

He didn't respond. The other two were all over him, concerned, but he was coughing and suddenly Nerys had a good idea what was going to happen, what had happened to all of them, and she *did not want to see this.*

But she did. Malïk was dying. And then, all three of them were running, shouting to one another they had had to go, had to get back to the city, and all of them were coughing and coughing and coughing and—

She stepped back from the pillar.

***

They began the walk back to their camp in silence, nothing but the darkness to keep them company. Finally, though, Nerys forced herself to explain what she'd seen.

They were halfway back when Seika stopped her, pointing to something on the ground, not far off.

"Nerys," she said. "Look."

It was a breather, identical to Nerys' in every way. She stepped over to pick it up, her feet crunching on the ice.

The fact that it wasn't in use meant its owner was almost certainly dead. She thought of the others, of her vision. Whose had it been?

She turned it over in her hands and tucked it into her bag. She was suddenly conscious of her own steady breathing, a rasping in and out through her breather. "We're going home now," she said and meant it this time. Seika had to understand.

"Why? If your breather was going to short circuit like that, wouldn't it have done it by now?"

"I'd rather not take that risk," Nerys said. "Of course, you're welcome to stay here and get yourself killed, instead." Though, to be fair, Seika's breather could be a different matter entirely; it wasn't part of the same set as the others. But she hoped after this, Seika would have a better sense of the dangers of wandering out here alone.

***

They stayed the night nearby. The entire time, Nerys worried over her breather. Several times, she found herself on the edge of sleep, when the thought came, unbidden, that the breather had broken, and she was taking her last gasp of air. Nerys took measured, careful breaths for several minutes before she felt safe trying to sleep again.

She was so close to death. The idea of her—of the abstract sentience that was *her*—just not existing was terrifying in a way she could never have expressed aloud. Nerys had known when she'd signed on that this was a possibility. But now that it was here and close, and her companions—her friends—were dead, she didn't know that she could take it.

Seika was asleep, lying beside her in her separate sleeping bag. Nerys didn't know what time it was; they were too far from Lumnis for the brilliant electric lights to shine in, and so here, there was no night and no day. Just dark and cold and black.

What she did know was that she was tired. She slept, eventually, but not well.

***

"What were your power lessons like, as a postcog?" Seika asked. Her footsteps echoed through the empty city streets as they walked.

"Incredibly boring," Nerys said.

They passed the time as best they could while heading home. Nerys found herself talking more and more as they continued. They dredged up shared memories of days past, and then

80

commiserated or laughed over these things that now felt so insignificant.

Every now and then Nerys would stop and pull out her map, and then they would continue on their way. It was printed on plant-fiber paper, and its edges were white and blank, distant areas yet to be explored. But the path back to Lumnis was clear, and that was what mattered.

As Nerys went to put it away, this time, she noticed something off about the dead breather she'd picked up from that site where she'd lost her expedition. Small green plant buds seemed to have sprouted from it, as if out of nowhere.

She understood.

Back in the old days of ice-wastes exploration, breather technology was often not as reliable as it was now. The life form that powered it had not yet been refined into what it was today, and there were records of early expeditions who never came back. There were records, too, of early expeditions who came back with small white flowers sprouting from their breathers, the device's planetoid organism forgetting all its careful training and growing too fast, too big for its space. They returned coughing and wheezing as the devices malfunctioned.

It had stuck in her mind since she'd first learned about it. But this hadn't happened for a long time—centuries if she remembered correctly. People still went missing, but that was how it went. Yet everyone was so sure the glitch had been fixed. What Nerys had seen, what Nerys was looking at now, seemed to suggest otherwise.

Would that happen to her and Seika? Would some future

scavenger stumble upon her flower-covered corpse, wondering what had happened?

**

It was a three-day trip back to Lumnis, and Nerys awoke on the morning of that third day to the sound of Seika coughing. It was too close to the sound of Malïk in her vision to be comfortable. Nerys sat up and looked at her, worry pulling at her mind like a fraying thread.

There were small green buds poking out of the metal edges of Seika's breather, so small Nerys wouldn't have noticed had she not known what to look for.

"Are you okay?" she asked after Seika had realized she was awake.

"I think so," she said, but her voice trembled, and Nerys wasn't sure whether this was due to the malfunction or fear.

"Let's get moving," she said, and they did.

They walked for a long while. Seika coughed occasionally but seemed otherwise fine.

Nerys started coughing, too. It was like getting grass stuffed into her mouth; little prickles of organic matter all over the inside of the device, and an unidentified *something*—petals, maybe, or pollen?—scratching at her throat and nose. It might have been no more than a nuisance if she hadn't known already what it meant.

Hours later, Seika stumbled, and Nerys grabbed at her to stop her from falling. "Nerys," Seika said, urgent, only it was so hard to make out the syllables through the plant matter that it barely sounded like her name at all. "I'm..." She didn't finish the sentence. She was looking at Nerys as if she had all of the solutions. She didn't.

"Can you breathe?" she said. Seika nodded. "All right, then. Keep walking forwards. I don't think it's far now." If she was right about anything this whole trip, let her be right about this.

Lumnis was visible, getting closer with each step, but it was hard to judge just how far that distance was, or how long it might take them to cross it. Or, for that matter, how long either of them had left.

Nerys put an arm around Seika to steady her, and she leaned most of her weight onto Nerys. She stumbled, every few steps, and Nerys pulled her back onto her feet, and then they kept going, two dying women making their last stand as best they could.

They could make it back. They had to. Her party had died, but that was because they hadn't been prepared. This would be different. They had *time*.

"Nerys?" Seika said.

"Yes?"

"What were you doing out here?" It was an unexpected question, but somehow it made sense.

"Scavenging," she said. "It was a job, Seika, that's all."

"Oh." She was quiet, grasping Nerys' arm for support. Nerys wondered if it was a good idea for her to be talking when she was having such difficulty keeping up her breathing. But she didn't say this aloud."I just wanted to see what it was like," Seika said. "I'm going to make priestess next month, and I just... I just wanted to do something, before I had all those *responsibilities*, you know?"

Nerys turned her head to look her in the face. "You were serious about that, back in the day? The priestess thing?"

"Yeah," Seika said. Nerys expected her to elaborate, but she didn't.

Nerys coughed. Seika, it seemed, was past coughing. Whether this was good or bad was unclear. Nerys was inclined to believe it was the latter.

The plant shoots' growth was slow and invisible, but it was happening. They were just going to keep getting larger and larger, pushing through the mechanics until the breathers were just useless, deadly chunks of metal strapped to their faces.

Nerys shuffled forward through the stone and ice and glass that blanketed the earth, practically carrying Seika along with her. She kept moving forward. For a long while, this was all she knew, just the onward motion of it.

She wondered, in the back of her head, if Luned and the others had made it this far. If they'd made it home. Or maybe they were just out there, still wandering. More likely not. Nerys had their best map, and the three of them could only have had so long before it was all over.

She and Seika could only have so long before it was all over, too.

At a certain point, Nerys realized she couldn't quite recall where they were going or why. She knew they were headed home, but she couldn't quite figure out how that made sense. She was freezing, and light-headed, and nauseous, but Seika was next to her, and her home city glowed brightly ahead of them. She kept moving. Forwards, forwards, forwards.

Then Seika did something unexpected: she *stopped* moving.

She whispered something that Nerys couldn't understand.

"We have to keep going," Nerys said. She didn't know if Seika could understand her, either. Did it matter? She could see Lumnis just ahead, shining with light. They were so *close*, they were *so close*. They couldn't stop now.

Seika collapsed.

Nerys caught her, but she looked—unconscious? She was still warm, at least, still breathing. Or Nerys *thought* she was still breathing. She wasn't quite sure.

"Come on." Her voice cracked.

Seika didn't respond. She didn't move.

Nerys looked at the distance left between them and the first small door to her home city, outlined in dark gray against the city lights

Nerys grabbed hold of Seika's unconscious body and began to drag her, her mind singing an endless refrain of her name.

She saw it play out all over again in reverse, through Seika's eyes.

The plants growing. The breathers malfunctioning. Her and Seika, both of them full of fear. Their long treks back and forth across Eloton, wandering and uncertain and in danger. Their meeting.

There was a spark of excitement in Seika at encountering Nerys, and then a low bitterness, and then the fear. Always, the fear. Things blurred and faded. Seika making her exit from Lumnis for the first time, Seika saying her goodbyes and promising she'd return.

Nerys saw all of this as she held tight to Seika, kept moving forward, closer and closer to home. She thought about Seika again and delved further back.

The days and weeks and years flew by, the reading made all the stronger by their shared history, and she saw herself, she saw the schoolroom, she saw the teacher marking the dividing line between different types of powers. Seika making a complaint, muttering something about even having to go to a tunnel school when they knew her family lived on the surface. Meeting Nerys, for the first time, all those years ago.

They met eyes. They avoided one another as best as they could.

***

Nerys took a breath of warm, fresh air as she stumbled past the airlock that led into the covered city. She dropped Seika to the floor not far beyond, and the door slid shut behind them, beginning the room's pressurization.

There was no one there waiting for them. She had opened the door herself, even as she'd hovered on that precipice of consciousness her visions took her to.

Nerys' breather, non-operational and bursting with flower buds, lay on the floor next to Seika's unmoving form. Hers had come off at some point during this last rush, tossed to the ground useless and covered in delicate blossoms.

Nerys leaned against the wall for a moment, catching her breath. She was on the border between home and the deadly place beyond, but it was so warm, here, compared to outside. Even now she was aware of the feeling returning to her thawing limbs. Her fingers seemed to be burning up, and her knowing this to be inaccurate did nothing to relieve the sensation of cold heat.

86

Nerys slid down to sit next to Seika on the floor. She shook her weakly. Seika didn't wake up.

"Seika," Nerys said. Seika made a soft, wordless sound, and opened her eyes. Nerys felt a tension within herself release. "Wake up," she said. "We made it."

The Mercenary

Beth McCabe

Beth McCabe is a proud resident of Tacoma, Washington. McCabe is a graduate of the Barnard College Creative Writing Program, where she placed second in the Elizabeth Janeway Fiction Prize. Her work has appeared or is forthcoming in Blue Monday Review, Halfway Down the Stairs, Liquid Imagination, Brilliant Flash Fiction, Highlights for Children, and other publications.

A ping in my ear indicated the sweet flow of money into my account. That would be the payment from the Transgalaxy MegaCorp for blowing up their competition a year before yesterday's hostile takeover. I blinked to flow the credits to my ID chip. I wouldn't have gotten them yet where I was going, and I'd need to stand some rounds of decent hooch.

Galactic bond traders don't drink the cheap stuff.

"Fred, I'm taking a week off," I told my chronobot.

"Where are you going, Amy?" Fred asked. "Proteus? Ceres?" He had a list of resorts in his data bank. Of course, I'd never been to any of them. Too busy working and saving every credit.

"Not where, Tin Man. When."

"Amy, you aren't using Guild resources for personal time travel, are you?"

"Uh huh."

Fred went through a series of rapid visual sensor blinks, his version of "Cannot compute." But all he said was, "OK, when are you going to?"

"June 14, 3142," I answered. "A week before Todd leaves me."

Fred wouldn't have been so docile if I hadn't disabled his reporting ware. I'd planned this mission for a long time, and no over conscientious polysteel puppet was going to get in my way. I noticed his little ovoid head twitching, though. Perhaps I hadn't done as good a job with the override as I thought.

I settled into my transfer pod, deep in memory. Eight years earlier my husband had told me he'd met someone else. "I'm so sorry, Amy," he'd said, crying like a little girl. Young Me ripped out my commlink and went on a bender. Then I entered the Chrono Guild to get access to time travel, enduring the most punishing, badass training program in the galaxy. To my surprise I turned out to be a pretty damn good mercenary. But I had never let go of my heartbreak – or my obsession.

My plan was simple. Like most nice guys, Todd was a sucker for people who lived on the dark side. If I went back with my ripped bod and 3D facial scarring, he'd have no idea who I was; even my voice had deepened. Once I'd gained his confidence I'd winnow out his girlfriend's identity. Then phhhhttt – kinetic slice to her jugular. Neat and discreet. That would at least give Young Me a second chance.

Of course, I was a little shaky on the details. Changing the fates of strangers was just business, but as Fred was attempting to remind me, the extensive Guild conditioning included a strong taboo against screwing with time for personal reasons. Who knew what would await me when I returned to my native time? But I was willing to take that risk.

Fred plugged the line into my inlet and started a dopa flow to soften the effect of the transfer nanos. I'd have to work fast once I got there, because the Guild had also built in a failsafe to make

90

sure we didn't linger in non-native time. After a week our cells began to degrade. And time sickness was an ugly way to die.

***

The place where the financial wizards hung out was all dark wood and real leather. It even had a human bartender. My kind didn't frequent places like this, but then, to my knowledge, nobody had ever thrown a Chrono out of a bar.

I spotted Todd immediately, laughing with his buddies, dark hair rumpled, tunic open. A couple of nervous dweebs hopped off their stools when they saw me coming. I straddled the seat next to Todd.

"Top-shelf for everyone, barkeep," I said. The guy took one look and got to work pouring without a word.

"Hey, thanks," Todd said. "You're a Chrono, aren't you?"

"Yup. I just popped a rival megacruiser out of orbit for a big client. It's spinning into infinity, and I'm flush as an Aegirian whore."

"Wow," he said. "I thought those ships were sabotage-proof."

"It's a long story."

I bought a few more rounds and entertained the boys with lurid tales of Chrono life. I didn't want to press my luck the first night, though, so I took off pretty early. "Maybe I'll see you around," I told Todd casually. "I'm looking for someone, and I hear he shows up here." Flimsy excuse to keep coming by. But not entirely untrue.

***

The next night he was back. All those times he'd stayed out he'd told Young Me he was working late, but after his confession I assumed he'd been with her. Apparently the answer was none of the above.

I walked up to the bar.

"Hey, I'm glad you're back," he said. "I owe you a drink or six."

I shrugged and sat. "Your wife OK with you closing down bars every night?"

"How'd you know I was married?"

Oops. "You just seem like the kind of guy who would be," I said.

"Yeah, I'm married. Kind of." He stared into the crystal blue liquid in his glass. "Amy's sweet, but she's a lightweight. She shops and she lunches. You know the type. Well, maybe you don't," he said, grinning at the tattoos shifting across my face. "And I'm sure you don't want to hear about my pansy-ass marital problems."

"You're right. I don't. Anyway, I bet you've got a hot girlfriend." Tell me her name, Todd.

"Nah. I'm too much of a straight arrow for that."

OK. He didn't trust me enough to confide in me yet. I still had time.

I hung out with him for the next few nights, but I couldn't find a way to turn the conversation back to his love life. Soon I began to experience the little bouts of the dizziness that herald time sickness. By the seventh night I was feeling the full effects: disorientation, migraines. I needed to leave before my cells went berserk. And I'd accomplished nothing.

"So," I said that last night, "my gig in this time is done. Gotta go back." I turned so he wouldn't see the tears welling in my darkened eye sockets.

To my surprise he reached for my hand. "Listen. I know this sounds weird, but I need to tell you something before you leave. I'm in love with you," he blurted.

Whoa. What?

"You're so strong," he said. "So different from my wife. But I think there's sweetness underneath the swagger." He took another swig of liquid courage. "I told Amy we were through before I came tonight. I don't know if you could be with someone as boring as me, but it wouldn't be fair to stay with her."

I took a deep breath. This wasn't the way it was supposed to go down, but Chronos were used to improvising. "Todd," I said, "I am your wife."

"What's that now?"

"It's me, Amy. From the future."

It was his turn to stare as I tried to arrange my feral appearance into something resembling Young Me's cheerful cluelessness. "Please don't say 'tell me something only Amy would know'," I said. "It's me. I became a Chrono so I could come back and vaporize the woman you left me for."

He wore the same confused look that Fred had when I told him I was going on a personal time jaunt. "Wait. How can you be her?"

"Chrono training changes you. A lot."

I could see he was starting to buy it. "So," he said slowly. "I left you for... you."

"And everything will work out," I said, hoping it was true. "Now you know Young Me doesn't have to be a fluffball. Go home and tell her you made a mistake. Help her become...me." I smiled. "Listen, though, if she still becomes a Chrono, tell her to forgo the beauty treatments from hell."

Todd was grinning. His eyes lost focus as he tried to contact Young Me on his commlink. "No answer."

"She'd have cut her link a while ago. But I can tell you that she's going to hang around drinking and crying for a good while."

He got up and kissed my tattooed lips, drawing stares from the other patrons. Then he headed for the door. "I love you," I called after him.

I needed to get to a Guild center for the transfer back. I was fading fast, and this time already had one Amy. I was downing a final shot for the road when I heard the blast. I shoved my way out of the bar and ran into the street. Todd lay there, his gut aerated by a couple of thugs who were digging out his ID chip. Reflexes kicked in and I killed them quickly. Then I dropped to the ground and cradled his body. I would have cried if I remembered how.

Back at the apartment, Young Me would be throwing things in a bag for her epic binge. Then she'd turn herself over to the Guild, never knowing Todd was dead. At least it looked like the timeline was more or less intact. So, in eight years, she would find out that she was the only woman he'd ever loved.

Twice.

The Watchers

Shelly Jones

Shelly Jones is an Assistant Professor of English at SUNY Delhi, where she teaches classes in mythology, literature, and writing. She received her PhD in Comparative Literature from SUNY Binghamton. Outside of academia, she is an active nerd who enjoys board games, Dungeons and Dragons, being outdoorsy, and knitting.

He did not know why he had agreed to marry her. For a long time he thought it was because she would hum at everything she did. She hummed while cooking. She hummed while cleaning and sewing. She hummed when she raked leaves and shoveled dirt and chopped firewood. She even hummed, or so he thought he heard over his own grunting, on the few occasions when they had consummated their union. Her humming was an intoxicating low rumble, a contralto line that lingered in the room even after she had left it. He remembered the first time he had heard her. They had been to a funeral service for the local baker, he with his mother and she alone, for all of her relatives had died when she was young. He had known this, of course, but it never really struck him until he saw her alone at the wake. How many other services had she attended as a girl for her family? She wore a grey smock and a thick wool coat, the color of new potatoes. While the other mourners stood silent with their heads bowed, clutching handkerchiefs or wordlessly mouthing prayers, she rocked gently, pushing her weight from one foot to the other and hummed a low, idle tune. But no one minded. No one thought her rude or obscene, though, for some reason, he feared they might. He could imagine an old, dour woman spitting on her, the thick mucus sticking to the wool, and calling her names for dancing and singing at the funerary rites. But no one seemed to even notice her. She was as much a part of the scene as a catbird in the tree or a period at the end of a sentence. Why, then, he had wondered, had he noticed her?

He never could answer this question. So many questions about her he could not answer. Or the answers changed as the years went on. But wasn't that part of every marriage? He could not know. He only knew the conditions and terms of his own. He thought about this as he sat in front of a beehive in the middle of the night, a cheerless moon gaping at him and his chapped hands and lips. It was beginning to get cold at night. He would need to wear gloves and a hat for his nightly ritual. She would provide these for him. She always did. Wasn't that enough?

The old men in the village would say, "Every man needs only a warm bed and a warm belly. And lucky is he who has someone to provide these for him." Hadn't she always kept him comfortable?

The older women in the village would smile at him on his way out of town each night as they sat balling up yarn or braiding rags of stained shirts and threadbare pants into rugs. "A good one, that one," they'd nod his way. "A man of his word is more valuable than next year's seeds." He wondered if he was just that. Had he kept his word, and what exactly had he said? He tried to remember.

After the funeral of the baker, he had left his mother chatting with the widow and followed the distant hum through the cemetery. He had to almost run to keep up with her loping pace. Breathless, he finally drew up the courage to address her, despite the fact that she was still twenty yards or so ahead of him.

"Why do you hum so for a funeral?" he asked, realizing halfway through the accusatory tone of his question.

98

She stopped under a bough of a great elm and turned toward him, placing her hand on the trunk as if needing to rest a moment. Her hip jutted out as her upper body seemed to fold into the tree and he was struck by how singular she was: an oak in the middle of a corn field, a burning bush in the middle of a green forest.

"Does it bother you?" she asked, wiping her brow with the back of her sleeve.

The man shifted his weight between his feet and removed his hat. "No," he said slowly, unsure of how to phrase his response. He felt as though her eyes were boring into him and he was not sure if he could stand under their gaze. "It does not bother me. I have never heard someone hum at a funeral before. Sing, yes, but not hum."

"Well," she said, patting the elm with the palm of her hand as if it were an obedient dog that should run along now. "Now you have." And she turned and strode away.

Leaping awkwardly at the sight of her back, the man stumbled forward, stammering. "Were, were you good friends with the baker?" He said, trying to interest her enough so she would stop again.

"No," she replied over her shoulder, her pace slowing, but constant.

"Why were you here then?" he asked bluntly, shocked by his own rudeness.

Stopping, she turned again. Her hazel eyes were narrow, too narrow for him to see the golden circle around her pupil.

"Is it a crime to pay one's respects for the dead? Has some law passed that I do not know about?"

99

"No, of course not, but..." he tried to explain.

"Then why do you ask me these questions?" her voice remained even and level despite the clear anger. She stood in the cemetery, backlit, and seemed to vibrate with annoyance.

"I... I have not seen you in town since we were both much younger. When, when your family...Your humming, it, it reminded me of something, made me notice you today. At the funeral. I only wanted to say, I suppose, that I would like to hear more."

At this she had simply nodded and gestured that he should follow her.

She had led him to the beehive that day. It was quiet, he thought to himself, quieter than it had ever been since. The beehive was located in a grove of myrtle by a pond a few miles from town. It was a large willow trunk with a plain board roof that had long ago warped with age. Her grandfather had probably built it, he surmised. The roof, the man saw, could be removed so the honey could be extracted from the hollow stump, where the bees nested. There must be more sophisticated systems out there in the world, he presumed, but this ancient design was clean and simple, easy for him to understand. For he knew nothing about bees.

"I have told the bees of the passing of the baker," she began to explain as if to herself. "He was a good man, who bought our honey faithfully for the past thirty years. My grandfather always spoke highly of him." She let her hand carefully rest on the wooden roof of the house-like hive. "They must be saddened at the news and are keeping to themselves today."

He wanted to ask her many questions: did she always speak to the bees? How long had she tended them? When did she take over her family's farm? He tried to remember the local gossip about her family. Like many in the farming village, her grandparents were a stoic couple, who never complained, but always worked and strove for the betterment of their small home—and that included the bees. At some point that fateful day, she would explain how the two of them would each take a turn, watching the bees, keeping them company—for bees, it was told, were a social, communicative sort that bonded with their keepers. So the grandmother would sit with them all day while the husband slept and at evening they would switch and he would guard the bees at night—blanketing the hive in the cold, marveling at the way the summer moonlight illuminated the veins on their paper wings. And when the grandfather would come home, he would be amazed at all the grandmother had accomplished at home in his absence: tomatoes and peaches canned and stored for winter, thick wool blankets washed and folded, a roast with root vegetables simmering, filling their home with an earthy aroma that melted any bitterness as he walked in from the night's work of watching the bees. She had told him all of this in her measured way—but even now he had trouble remembering their conversation. What exactly had she said? What did he surmise or know from the gossip in town? Yet he could remember every detail, every point of her story—but how had she said it? Her family, including her grandparents, had died when she was young, he knew this without question. But she had not explained how and he had never asked her. Some of the older men in town had said it was an accident, a queer twist of fate that miraculously spared her. The women clucked their tongues at the loss and shook their heads in silence, eyes pinched closed as if warding off the gruesome memory.

Younger boys, who had nothing better to do than spin tales, had said his wife was a witch who had killed her whole family when they discovered her mystical secret and tried to kill her. The boys, awkwardly spitting tobacco juice so it would run down their hairless chins, had predicted that she would one day kill the whole town if they weren't careful. He understood why they would think this. In the years after her family had passed on, she had become reclusive, despite her young age of twelve, probably out of sheer necessity to keep the farm and the bees alive and thriving. She had to do all the work of three men and four women herself now alone—there could be no time for socializing, for dances, for idle conversation after church or while paying a bill at the dry goods store. She had lived that way for ten years before the baker's death, before he heard her in the cemetery.

"Probably why she hums to herself so much, trying to fill the quiet any way she can," he spoke the realization aloud, as if sharing it with the bees.

Still. He was not sure what had inspired him so that moment to ask her to marry him: whether it was the nostalgia of her hard-working ancestors, or the solitude of the beehive that day, or the way her eyes seemed to change hue when she hummed. Whatever the reason, he had placed his hand on top of hers on the cold wooden hive and asked if she would accept him, though he had nothing to give her. Although he did not want to admit it to himself, the man, he knew, was lame. He could not walk steadfast behind an ox-drawn plow, or carry milk and eggs from town to town, or even stand tall at a printer's press in the village. His profession thus far had been that of a misfit, a wretch, that kindly, pious folk took pity on. They would not insult him with charity, but gave him odd jobs like counting chickens after a fox attacked a local coop, or sorting buttons at the seamstress shop, or alphabetizing all the letters for the newspaper office after a small earthquake rocked and jumbled their sleepy town a few years back.

"You must follow in the way of my people," she said without looking up at him.

"What would I do?" he asked. He had heard of folks who tended to bees, of course, but it never occurred to him to ask what exactly they did. Would he have to count the bees? Keep track of how many flew out to find pollen and how many remained to work and create and produce the honey? Or to defend their queen? And how did they make honey anyway? The more the man thought, the more worried he had become. Could he do this? The woman smiled gently at his wide eyes. "You must befriend the bees," she spoke simply, clearly, her voice smooth and unwavering. "We must tend to the bees in shifts, for bees will learn to trust their keeper and remain true to you with time."

"But we will never see each other if you are with the bees during the day and I care for them at night," he had protested, drawing back to confront her with his logic.

"If you are with our bees, then you are near to me," she only replied quietly, her eyes fixed ahead.

"But how much tending do bees really need? Aren't they wild creatures who take care of themselves? Shouldn't we simply harvest it and let the bees alone? How much money could we make at the market for their honey?" he asked, still unsure of his future bee-keeping duties.

"Our honey," she corrected him.

At this he squeezed her hand gently and felt the sticky residue of honey on her skin.

And so it was done.

They had returned to the cemetery that day and met with the

103

reverend who had performed the funerary rites earlier in the morning. His mother had to be called for at their home for she had given up on waiting for her son's return. She was delighted at the prospect of his marriage and kissed his forehead three time for luck. He could not remember what she had given his bride or if they had even smiled at one another that day. Had she even said her vows? He could not remember. He could only remember the sweet smell of her when they embraced on the sunless day in the cemetery. And the first of many long walks back to the bees.

The men in the village would approve the match: a hard-working girl with a duty-bound man. "One with direction and one with blind strength, that is what is needed for the plow."

The women in the village would cry for their meager living and rip geranium leaves, throwing them off their porches in the direction of the new couple to soak up any evil lurking in their path.

After the first six months of their marriage, the old women in town had said, "You must be patient. The heavens reward those who wait." After a year of marriage, the old men in town had presented him with a small jug of cider and a sack of eggs with a nod and handshakes all around.

Embarrassed, he had taken the fertility gifts to the beehive and drank his shame away. The next year the old women handed him a special herbal tea that they must both drink before the deed and after. "A baby is always made with this," they had promised with a reassuring squeeze of his hand.

He had taken the tea home and handed it to his wife. She only laughed at the old women's impertinence.

He had wanted to ask why, why she wasn't with child, to accuse her of some treachery. But seeing her there, smelling the tea and boiling a pot of water, humming quietly, he knew it was not her fault. He had taken the tea from her and kissed her and waited for her kiss back. And when it came, they sunk to the floor, the tea leaves scattered beneath them. And when he was done, he returned to the bees, hoping to soon tell them that their keeper would be a father. But weeks passed, and he could not tell them any such news.

When five years passed without any new bundles in their home, the man gave up hope. The children in town, overhearing the disapproving tone in their parents' gossip, called the woman unnatural, the man a gelding. Another five years passed and no one bothered to say anything about it anymore.

She, for all the gossip and all the jeers, did not seem bothered at all.

But he, he could not still his brain.

And in the starry solitude of his nightly task, he would ask the bees for their advice. Should he continue to try? Continue to sleep with her despite the uselessness of the act? Should he even want a child? Could he care for one? He longed for a baby of their own, a child to raise and teach and prove his usefulness to the town—something tangible to contribute. They had been together for ten years with no luck. He tried to remember his own father, a dim, vague memory of a burly man with a mustache who never came in from the rain and died at the bottom of a mine. Could he provide for a child? Was he providing for his wife? These questions skittered along the pool of his mind, casting ever-widening fears and dreads that sent waves of panic through him.

And the bees, tucked in their hive, would murmur and hum, soothing his fractaled mind.

He sat with his knees bent in front of him, arms hugging his legs, as he pondered his wife. She was a good wife, really. And most men that he knew would covet aspects of his life: solitude, the comforts of home without the wifely needling, the griping, as they would say. As he was never home and awake when she, too, was also home. They each took shifts caring for and watching over the bees. Or at least, that's what they agreed to. For his part, he knew very little about bees and honey and apiaries. And so he did not so much as do anything during his long shift in front of the bees. Sometimes he would take a sweeping walk around the hive, lapping them in ever-widening circles until he could no longer hear their great din and he would worry, quickening his pace back to them. He did not know why it was so important that he remain there, close by, but whenever he strayed too far, he was seized with a dread of the bees, of his wife's silent disappointment, of failure, of the creeping feeling of death that would seize his legs. Other days he would bring a scrap of paper that had a few lines scrawled on it. In the evenings when twilight's dim glow still emitted light if not heat, he would sit with his paper and try to read. He would sit cross-legged, his back bowed, drooping over the sheet in his lap, studying the letters, trying to make sense of them. Now and then a bee, legs swollen with pollen would land on the paper. He would, at first, tense in fear and slowly rear back from the text, but then, once he realized the bee would not harm him, he followed it with his eyes as it strolled across the line, guiding him from one word to the next. His eyes focused on the bee and then on the inky smudge beneath its hairy feet. Peering through its papery wings, he was able to focus and discern each letter and then each word.

Once, on a particularly muggy evening, he had nodded off, his beard thick with sweat. And when he awoke, groggy and burdened by the air itself, he discovered a small creature on his knee. A white squirrel with black glassy eyes and fine thread-like whiskers sat staring at him. Its nose twitched as if smelling the salty-sweet patina of stale beer and sweat on his face. He watched the little animal, paws bent at its chest like an old man lazily rubbing his belly before yawning for bed. He admired the lithe fingers with thin, harsh claws protruding from its fur. He wondered what it would be like to touch it. He wanted to reach out his finger to the squirrel, a gentle, friendly gesture. Like giving your hand to a baby to squeeze in its fist and kick its legs in wide-eyed excitement. Would this squirrel, who squatted so attentively on his knee as he sat on the soft earth before the beehive, would she take his finger in her two paws, cradling it in her claws or touching his skin with the soft pads of its palm? As the squirrel's nose twitched, its whiskers springing up and down with each wrinkle, the man held his breath and thought about his wife. For a moment, he could not really picture her. She was a blur in his mind as he gazed at the pale squirrel and shivered. The convulsion of his body jolted the squirrel and it leapt off his knee and darted a few yards away before turning back. At first, the man thought he had befriended the creature and it was looking back at him, for confirmation, for recognition, to reassure him. But as he sat there staring, he realized that the squirrel was not looking at him, but at the beehive beyond him. Its usual gentle hum had multiplied and amplified to a drone and then a roar as thousands of bees emerged.

He had seen swarms of locusts in his youth dive and arch and skip one field only to land and ravage a neighboring plot. He had seen flocks of starlings drip across a sky, folding on a wing as though a single bird. But he had never, until then, and not since, seen a swarm of bees. It had not even occurred to him that this was something he should fear. And fear, despite the moon-eclipsing wall of bees that roiled before him, was not what he felt. Awe surged within him as the swarm swept to bend forward to inspect him and then, in a fluid, wave-like motion, seized upon

107

the unsuspecting animal. In a moment the white squirrel was lost in a funnel of howling bees and when the swarm quieted a moment later, and, exhausted, returned to the hive for the night, the little animal was gone.

He sat, transfixed, staring at the spot in the grass where she had been, as if trying to will the small white being back into existence. For a brief moment he wondered if the bees had somehow magically whisked the squirrel into the hive with them for safekeeping. But the childish hope quickly faded and he realized it was dead. Tears rimmed his eyes as he felt a barely perceptible weight gently press on his knee. He gasped, hoping to see the wondrous squirrel greeting him, but was mortified to see a single bee perched on the stiff wool of his pants. He wanted to strike at it, to swat it away from him, to crush it in his palm and feel its life juices trickle down his wrist. But he did not move. He could not move thinking of the natural force tucked away in the hive just beyond his reach. The single bee squatted there, its wings pressed back taut against its body. He could feel each of its legs, thin wisps of muscle, begin to give way as the bee slowly crawled up his leg. It moved methodically, each leg stepping in syncopated intervals, up his thigh and past his waist to his belly. Mesmerized by the bee, he sat, his legs tensed, his breath caught in the back of his throat. The sensation of the bee's tiny limbs, its hairy feet and piercing claws gingerly splaying across his stomach, overwhelmed him. He could feel the bee's antennae pressing, searching, feeling out for the right spot, tasting the soft flesh of his belly through his flannel shirt. His body arched as the bee pressed forward, its thorax expanding with each breath. He could feel the tension, the exquisite hunger of the bee as it suddenly stopped just above his navel. It stared at him, a subtle hum pushing forth from its vibrating body, as its barbed stinger sprung forth and into his belly. He had never been stung by a bee before and at first he did not feel pain. Wonderment overwhelmed his senses

108

as he tried to understand what had just happened. He threw his head back as the pain washed over him, the venom releasing into his blood. A roar of noise crashed into his ears; the hive groaning before him, buzzing frantically as the single bee, in a life-taking motion, ripped itself away from the man, its stinger and more left behind on his belly. It collapsed to the ground, shrinking under its wings, its legs kicking aimlessly in the air. With its last shudder, the hive quieted, stilled, and went silent. He, rubbing his stomach as if wiping away the wound, sat staring at the hive, his other hand protectively cupping the body of the dead bee.

He never spoke to his wife about his nights with the bees. Nor did she tell him what happened during her daily watchings.

He was surprised when he first noticed that her stomach was engorged. He had not noticed the subtler, more nuanced signs of her pregnancy: the gentle bowing of her hips, the nesting instinct that made her organize their home evenly, meticulously. As she stood before him, bending over to add wood to the fire, he tried to remember the last time they had been together. But the days and weeks and months of the same routine, the same restless watching in the dark, blurred in his mind and he could not remember.

"How long?" he asked, his voice a mixture of apprehension and joy. For so long they had wanted a baby, wanted something else in their lives to love. But now? Wasn't it too late? Wasn't he too old? He thought about the squirrel from the summer. He could not protect it. How was he supposed to protect a child?

"In the spring," she replied, wiping soot and sap from her hands with a cloth.

"How will our life change?" he asked quietly. It was an odd question, he knew, but a pertinent one. Would they continue their rotations? Would she still be able to watch the bees, or would he have to take over her chores? He imagined, some warm spring day in the future, when their son might accompany her to the hive: mother and child cutting through the bright pink branches of the myrtle grove, the bees heavy and sated with pollen. It made him warm to think about, but there was much to do before then.

She did not seem perturbed by the question, but tugged on her coat, which could just barely button, and smoothed the wool over her belly. "We will see," she said, and walked out the door to the bees.

He slept fitfully that day, his mind awash with questions. And when he returned that night to the bees, they were quieter, stiller, as though deep in their own thoughts.

"What should I do?" he asked aloud, his breath forming in front of him in the cold.

But the bees would not answer him.

Once, upon his return home, he discovered a pair of horns propped up against his doorstep. Angrily he grabbed the horns, a thin layer of ice cracking under his grasp. He wanted to shout, to rail against his meddling neighbors, to scream into their judging faces. But he did not. Instead he simply flung the discarded deer antlers into the woods and walked inside.

But the anger that he would not let out, would not set free, burrowed its way into their home, like a rodent, like a parasite. He did not speak to her for the rest of the winter. He did not want to believe that the child was not his, but how could it be? For ten years they had been married, had occasionally laid together, with no child. How could he believe, without question, without apprehension, that the thing growing in her was fully his? Their child? There was no such thing. Even the town knew that apparently.

He considered leaving, leaving her, leaving their bees, leaving the pending baby. But what would he do instead? He could not work. He knew no life other than this: the nocturnal watching of bees. And so he remained, fulfilling his promise in body only. He would return to the bees and sit there silent, staring, willing the hours to quicken their excruciatingly slow pace to no avail. He had grown tired of the bees, of his nightly routine, the emptiness of it. But still he remained.

And the bees grew listless, withdrawn. Their hive was cold to touch and in the snow-filled skies, no bees emerged.

One still, frozen evening, when he sat in the hollowed-out trench of snow to escape the fierce wind that whipped through trees and froze birds shivering on the limbs, he began to drift to sleep only to be awakened by a gentle hum. In his dreaming mind, he thought his wife, heavy with child and her thick winter coat, had come to visit him for the first time. She laid down next to him in the ice-crested depression, her cold nose pressing sharply into his neck, a chilling sensation that jolted him awake. He felt at his neck, a hum still spiraling in his ear, to discover a single bee. Carefully, he removed it, examining it in the palm of his hand. He wondered why it would escape from its warm hive into the frigid night. Was it lonely? Did it need his company? Was it afraid of the dark, of winter, of dying? Was this what it would be like to be a father and hold a frightened child in his arms after a nightmare? He watched its thin wings trying desperately to beat back the wind, to stay secure in his hand. And then he thought of the bee on his chest, the swarm. He thought of the albino squirrel, wondrous and consumed by the bees.

Almost impulsively, he balled up fingers into a fist, crushing the bee before it could sting him. He opened his fist and wiped the smeared bee remains on his pant leg before rolling over to sleep once more.

One day in the spring, he returned home, his boots crunching through the frost-covered grass. He heard a robin singing above him as he walked, and smiled. His son would be born soon, he realized. Someday he would teach him bird songs, the phases of the moon. He smiled again at this thought and walked into the quiet house.

His stomach emptied when he saw the baby on the floor, swollen and pale, the color of lime on a field on a grey November day. It did not occur to him to try to save the child for he knew he was gone before he could cross the room. As he drew closer, he noticed its eyes were caked in a thick smear of honey. Something she must have learned from her mother, he thought. A way to lock in its soul, perhaps.

How do we learn these acts, these rites that tie us from this life to the many before, he wondered. He could remember nothing from his father, no specific lesson or chore, and yet his mother had told him he held his fork the same way, he sniffed the air after a thunderstorm the same way, a look, a gesture, all the same. Who had she learned from, he wanted to know. She was alone for so long. Perhaps, he thought, there are simply some things women know instinctively, by feel at the first kick, the first blood, the first wave of labor. Had the baby cried, he wondered. Had it suffered? Had she?

He sank down over the little swollen bundle and rocked it in his arms. Its skin felt cold and rubbery like a bald tire against his face.

Thinking perhaps she had returned to the beehive, he hurried there, his bum leg aching with the exertion. But when he pushed back the myrtle branches, just beginning to leaf into a vibrant green, he saw and heard no bees.

How had she done it? How had she convinced the bees to follow her? He tried imagining her as a bee general, standing in front of the bees humming to them a rallying cry, ordering them to march behind her over the hills until they could find a new home. But this militant woman was not his wife. Perhaps not a soldier, but a sorceress, captivating the bees to follow her and leave their ancestral hive behind. He imagined her playing a pan-pipe made of honeycomb, thick globs of wax sticking to her upper lip. She would be beautiful in the lurid power, a force beyond recognition. This too, he realized, with a sigh, was not his wife. In the silence of the empty hive before him, he stooped in the realization that he did not really know her.

Some men in the village told him that bees will migrate when the vegetation is poor. "We had a hard winter and a late frost. There will be nothing for them to pollinate here."

Some women in the village told him that bees have very special bonds with their keepers, like that of a child to her parent. "They followed their ma," they say. "Let her have them, the poor dear. It's hard for a woman to lose her babe. She needs the bees," they said.

He sat staring at the hive wishing it would hum to life with the twitching energy of the bees. Or if they could not return, he thought, he wished that he might break apart into a million restless bees and swarm the world in search of her, humming her name into the wind.

The Red Tree

Natasha Suri

Natasha Suri is a librarian and has the cat to prove it. She moonlights as a writer, and lives in London.

The men were already in the newsagent's when Alder woke. She'd been dreaming of eating soil, her mouth packed with dirt, her stomach working itself into thorny knots. She'd woken up with a shudder, her body straining to be sick. But the noise of windows breaking convinced her to force the nausea back. She clamped a hand over her mouth and curled up into a ball. Hidden in the high branches of her tree, the men couldn't see her, but she could see them.

Big men. Big shoulders. They hadn't gone hungry.

Alder listened to the men rip apart the shop. She turned her wrist over, holding her watch to the light. She counted the minutes. She heard the scuffle of feet, a muffled noise, and carefully peered down.

A young man sat under the shade of her tree, crying. While the rest of the men continued to smash shelves in the newsagent's, he crouched in the dirt sobbing with his fist between his teeth so they wouldn't hear him. His shoulders were shaking with the force of it.

Alder watched him from up in the branches and weighed up the risks of trying to take his hammer from him. He'd left it on the ground by his right foot. If she jumped down she'd have half a second, at most, to pick the hammer up and smash in his skull. If she miscalculated--if he had a chance to shout for help, or grab the hammer before she could--she would be the one to die.

Alder didn't like the odds. Bodies were so fragile, after all. She decided to stay where she was. After ten minutes passed the man got to his feet and wiped his face on the back of his sleeve. He pulled his sleeve down over his hand to hide the teeth marks. Then he kneeled down, picked up his hammer, and walked away.

She heard one of the men shout. Then she heard the meaty slap of a fist. She placed her hands over her ears and waited for silence.

She waited another hour in the end, timing herself using the tick of her wristwatch. Then she climbed down and went in the newsagent's. The desk was broken and the metal shelves were on the floor, ripped off of their hinges. The elderly man who owned the shop lay dead behind the broken countertop, his head soft and blown wide. The beer was all gone, the packets of crisps and the bottles of water too. But the men hadn't taken all the chocolate bars, so Alder took one for herself and ripped open the packaging with her teeth.

When she turned to leave she saw the spider plant that usually sat in the window lying on the floor in a pool of its own dirt and broken glass, its roots exposed to the air. Alder picked it up and tucked it in the crook of her arm like a baby, lifting her jacket and her shirt so it could feel her bare skin. "You can stay with me for now," she told it. It burrowed against her, slowly worming its way under her dermis. The green susurrated softly in greeting.

Alder wondered if anyone would come and bury the man, and then decided it was unlikely. He should have left a long time ago, when everyone else in the city had left. But he'd

116

been old and alone and he'd loved his shop. He'd liked Alder. He'd given her watch and had showed her to wind the tiny hands to the right time. *These are better than digital,* he'd told her. *They don't wear out.*

Alder thought about burying him. But she couldn't. All the good soil left belonged to the tree, and the rest of it was parched and hard, impossible to shift with the few tools she had available to her. She supposed she could cremate him, but she didn't like fire. He would have to remain where he was.

She took another chocolate bar and chewed on it slowly as she climbed back into her tree to wait. She watched the sun fall, and the fires start on the distant edges of the city, very far from home. She slept and this time she was careful not to dream.

***

When Alder woke it was night, deep black night, and it was too dark for her to see her wristwatch. But she could see the bright flame of a lit matchstick down below her. When she leaned forward she saw the young man's face haloed in the light. His left eye was swollen shut.

"Come down," he said.

Alder shook her head. Then, realising he could barely see her, she said, "No."

"You can't stay here," the man said. "They're going to come back. They'll find you."

"You killed the old man in the shop," said Alder. Talking made her throat hurt. She wasn't used to it. "You used your hammer."

"I didn't hurt him," he said. "They hurt him. The others." His voice wobbled. "It was horrible."

When Alder said nothing, the man swore and blew the matchstick out before it could burn his fingers. Fumbling in his pockets, he lit another and held it up so he could see her.

"I've run away," he said. "I'm trying to get to the Castle. You could come with me. We might make it together."

"I want to stay here," said Alder.

"You can't. They're following me. They'll find you."

"They may not find me," Alder pointed out.

"If you stay here, *someone* will find you in the end," he said desperately.

"I'm waiting for someone to find me," said Alder. "So that seems reasonable."

"You might be found by-- someone bad. Not someone you want to be found by. And I... I can take you somewhere safe." His voice grew smaller. "Please don't make me go alone."

Alder leaned forward and looked at him hard. His one good eye was very big in the dark. She'd been fooled by his height, but now she looked closer she could see his hands and feet were too big for him, his skin soft, his face an open carapace.

"You're not a man, are you?" said Alder. "You're just a boy."

He didn't protest. "Please," he said.

Alder considered her options. The spider plant rustled against her ribs thoughtfully. The green began to whisper all at once, sending a susurration through her whole body, head to toe. She shivered, and decided.

"I don't like fire."

The matchstick had almost burned down to his fingers again. "Fine," he said, and blew it out. "Will you come down now?" he said into the dark.

Alder nodded, then remembered--again--that he couldn't see her. "Yes," she said. She kissed the branch of her tree. *Be safe*, she thought. A little kernel bloomed under her sternum in response, and Alder took it on gladly. She jumped down.

The boy was shivering. She thought of the spider plant lying on its side with its roots exposed, and took his hand.

"Show me the way to the Castle," she said.

***

The Castle and Hound was an old pub set at the top of a hill. There were still flower baskets hanging from the eaves and a sign announcing the pub's name, but the sign had split down the middle and the baskets were empty. It was a dump. Apart from the addition of a figure standing on the roof pointing a hunting rifle down at them, it looked like every other abandoned building Alder had ever seen.

Alder stopped dead in her tracks when she saw the rifle, but the boy gave a gasp and let go of her, running through gaping fence to the pub door.

"It's me!" he yelled. "It's me! Let me in!"

The gun lowered and the figure vanished. A moment later the door opened. Alder raced after the boy, tumbling with him through the door. A woman with a hunting rifle still slung over her shoulder slammed the door shut and barred it behind them.

"Were you followed?" the woman asked urgently.

"I don't know," the boy gasped, but the woman was no longer listening. She hugged him tight and said, "Matthew, oh Matthew, I thought you were dead. You foolish boy. How could you leave me?"

"I thought they'd teach me how to be strong," the boy said, crying again.

"I told you," she said. "I told you the world can't be trusted anymore. I told you but you never listen! And who on earth have you brought with you?"

The woman was still talking, asking questions, but Alder was no longer listening to her. She looked around the pub, at the tables and chairs stacked against the walls, at the carpet and rolled back to leave the floorboards bare. She got down onto her hands and knees and smelled the dust and resin and blood that had settled there. Her heart began to hammer. Her mouth dried up.

"Someone is a witch," said Alder. The boy and the woman fell silent. "Someone has put blood and dreams into the floor." She pressed her cheek to the floorboards and looked up at the two humans still clutching each other. "Where can I find the witch?" she asked urgently. "You must tell me. I have to know."

"Who are you?" asked the woman.

"I saved her," the boy said proudly, and Alder didn't bother to correct him.

"The witch," she said again. "I need to speak to her. Please."

The woman carefully untangled herself from the boy and moved to stand in front of him, protecting him from Alder's sight. She hadn't reached for her rifle yet, but probably only because she was too close to Alder to put it to its intended use. Her eyes were as dark and deep as earth after rain.

"I'm the witch," the woman said. "Now, tell me who you are."

"I'm the one you summoned," said Alder. "I was waiting for you. Why didn't you come for me?"

The witch stared at her for a very long moment. Then she said, "Oh. Oh my God."

***

The witch told Alder to call her by her name. Her name was Laura.

Laura brewed a pot of tea over a camper stove and poured out two mugs. She gave one of them to Alder and warned her not to drink it until it cooled.

"Do you need to drink?" the boy asked. "And eat?"

"Don't ask questions like that, Matthew," said the witch. "It's rude."

"Sorry."

"I don't have to," said Alder. "But I like to. I like chocolate especially."

"Me too," the boy said, pleased.

"You need to go to away now, Matthew," said the witch. "Before I remember how angry I am at you."

"But Laura-"

"*Now.*"

Matthew scuttled off, and Laura propped her arms on the bar and looked at Alder steadily. "Tell me everything you remember. I need to know."

"I remember waking up underground," Alder said. That was her first memory: the soil in her mouth, loamy and wet. The terror of it pressing down on her new body, so fragile and full of bones. "I remember not wanting to wake up. I was somewhere else, and then I was flesh, and there was a witch calling to me. *Live*, she told me. So I decided I would."

She could have chosen not to. She could have chosen to remain in her tree, dreaming sap and root and water dreams, bloodless and sweet. But the terror in the witch's voice had made her curious. *Live. Please. Live.*

So she had.

"I dug myself out from under the roots of my tree. It was night and the world was burning. I was very afraid." She swallowed. "But I waited for you. I thought you would come and get me. I waited a long time."

"And there was only you? No one else arrived with you?" asked Laura. "Nothing—grew?"

"Just me."

"Well," Laura said. She pressed her fingertips hard to her forehead and squeezed her eyes briefly shut "Well. I've dragged you into a mess, and I'm sorry for it."

The witch explained then, that she had tried to perform a spell to bring the plants back to life. But the plants hadn't returned. All over the city they had kept on burning and rotting and dying in their droves just like everything else, and the witch had thought her spell had failed. Then Matthew had run away, and run back, and brought Alder with him.

"My mum always told me to be careful with new spells. 'They go wrong' she said. 'They never work like you expect them to.'" Laura shook her head. "I should have listened to her."

"Yes," Alder agreed. "But I'm here now, and I suppose I don't mind being alive." The bar was old mahogany, covered in grooves. Alder reached across it and covered the witch's hand with her own. "You're warm," Alder said. "Did you know how wonderful it is, how warm you are, how flesh feels?"

Laura stared at her for a long time. Then she drew her hand back.

"You should sleep," she said. "I'll be on the roof if you need me."

***

Alder lay on the floor for two hours. She couldn't sleep.

She went in search of the witch. It didn't take her long to find a hatch that led to the roof. She climbed up and found Laura crouched on the shingles, holding her rifle.

The moon was out. In its faint light, Laura's dark skin looked grey.

"I saw one of the men," Laura said grimly. "I knew they'd come."

Alder sat down next to her. She propped her chin up on her knees.

"You can shoot one," she said.

"If I have to."

123

"You can't shoot all of them."

"No," Laura said. "No, I can't. You're right."

"Can you use your magic to get rid of them?"

"I don't have much left in me," Laura admitted. "I should never have tried to bring back the trees. I used myself up. It'll come back in time, but we don't have much of that, I think."

"No," Alder agreed. She looked down at her watch. Time was ticking away.

The witch swallowed. "I was trying to wake the world back up," she whispered, looking down at the rifle in her hands. "But there was nothing left to wake up, I suppose. Just you." She looked up at Alder again then with bleak eyes. "The world is dead, isn't it? It's too late."

Alder shrugged. "I don't know."

"It doesn't matter anyway." The witch's shoulders slumped. "The men Matthew ran off will be here soon, and I won't be able to fight them off for long. Fool boy. I should never have taken him in."

"You could send him away again."

Laura shook her head. "It's too late for that. And besides, I love him. It can't be helped." She exhaled slowly, straightening her spine with visible effort. "You should go before they come. Those men are dangerous. You won't want to face them. You'll want to be somewhere safe."

Alder looked at Laura's solemn face, her straight eyebrows and the hard set to her jaw. Alder thought of the men with their hammers, the men with their fists who didn't like it when boys cried.

She thought of the old man who'd given her the watch on her wrist, his head soft and pulverised, all its redness spilled. She stood up.

"Come down to the garden with me," she said. "I want to show you something."

***

"The old man who owned the shop by my tree loved plants," said Alder. She shrugged off her oversized jacket. "When they started to die, he asked me to save them. So I did."

She took off her shirt and her trousers, which had fit her just as badly as the jacket. She toed off her shoes. Naked apart from her watch, she stepped out under the bare sky where the moonlight could touch her. Laura watched her from the Castle's doorstep, rifle steady in her hands. The witch sucked in a sharp breath when Alder turned to face her, naked and bristling with life.

"This was the first one I took from him," Alder said, pointing to her thigh. "A rose. And here..." she gestured to her stomach. "These were nettles. I chose to save those."

She described each inch of her body, each green thing she'd kept and saved on her own skin. She pointed to the fronds etched against the flesh of her ribcage. "This was the last plant I took from him, when the men killed him." She moved her fingers to her sternum, and touched the small seed centred there, pulsing with new life. "And this is a gift from my tree. My last gift."

"Look at you." The witch sounded dazed. She didn't move as Alder curled her toes into the ground and looked out at the city, which was still dark and poisonous with burning.

"The soil isn't so bad here," said Alder, as the green fluttered and shifted under her skin. "Your magic protected it a little. This is as good a place as any to give them a home, I think." She looked back at the witch. "I could grow my new tree here," said Alder thoughtfully. "I could grow a whole forest. The men wouldn't be able to reach you through that."

"Oh please," said the witch. There were tears running from her eyes. "Oh please, do. Do."

Alder kneeled down. The green shivered, terrified and delighted as she set her fingers against earth.

It's time, she told it. *Don't be afraid now. You need to wake up. I can't be your home any longer.*

She learned forward and kissed the ground. Life sprang from every inch of her skin, burrowing into the earth, bursting its way through clods of soil. The witch had poured magic into every inch of the Castle: spells for protection, incantations for invisibility, curses to keep her enemies at bay. Her magic had been made of love and blood and dreaming, and the green fed on it as all life feeds on such things.

Alder's skin was stretched thin. Suddenly exhausted, she tried to stand up and found herself stumbling. The witch caught her before she collapsed entirely. Laura helped her gently down to the ground. She lay Alder's head in her lap.

"My God," Laura said, over and over again. She was still weeping. "My God, just look at that."

Alder felt as if they stayed there for a very long time, watching plants sprout to fierce life, watching the kernel of her tree grow larger and larger still, until it threatened to blot the moonlight from the sky. She wanted to look at her watch and count the passing minutes, but her wrist felt too heavy to lift. So she counted in her head instead, and pressed her cheek against Laura's thigh.

"It looks like your spell worked after all," Alder observed.

"Yes," Laura said. Her voice was thick. "I suppose it has." She touched Alder's hair with trembling fingers. "Don't fall asleep," she said. "I'm afraid..." the witch's voice trailed off.

"Afraid?" Alder prompted, confused.

"Afraid that you won't wake up."

"Oh," Alder said. "Don't be afraid of that."

She closed her eyes, let out a breath, and died.

***

The witch dug a hole under Alder's tree. It was a good tree. Deep roots, generously soft soil. The witch wrapped Alder in sheets studded with sunflowers and whispered prayers against her ear. She kissed Alder on the forehead, tucked the sheet over her face, and began to bury her.

It was a good death.

Under the soil, Alder stretched out her roots. She felt the good soil, the sweetness of it. If she'd had the lungs for it, she would have laughed with joy.

She'd told the witch not to be afraid, and she'd meant it. Alder had never felt more alive or more awake. The green was all around her, blooming into hungry, childish new life. She could feel the pulse of it as if they were still one body, one lovely symbiotic creature again.

The green had begun dreaming restless dreams. Not good green-dreams of cold sap and sun like it had dreamt before she had been its soil, but flesh dreams, red and wet. It was dreaming her rage and her anger; dreaming the tick of a watch, the sound of a hammer breaking bone. It dreamt Laura's face, wet with tears. The green was wrathful, hungry, confused.

This is how humans dream, she told it, by way of apology. *That's why they make everything burn.*

They'd lived too long together, she and the green. Neither of them were really quite human or quite green any longer. When Laura had turned over the soil, it had been red and wonderfully warm. The roots of Alder's tree had been sinewy with muscle. And Alder, for all her flesh was dead and she was tree and root and leaf again, could still feel the softness of Laura's lips on her forehead and the corresponding winged swoop of her own stomach like the ghost of her flesh remained with her still.

The green was shaking off its dreams. It was waking up. She felt its gnarled roots settle, deep and strong with fury; shivered as thorns bristled viciously to the surface of vines and flower stems, as the earth softly gave away, shaping itself into ready traps. It was knew what the men had done. It wouldn't fail her.

Laura had not climbed back up onto the roof. She kneeled on Alder's new grave, her rifle on the ground beside her. The trees of Alder's red-green forest towered above her, dark and austere, great branches lifting their leaves up to the sky in a jewelled halo. She was murmuring the sort of prayers humans pray when someone had died for them. Then she leaned forward, pressing her lips to the soil, praying to it the way witches pray.

"Kill them," she whispered. "Holding them at bay isn't enough. You feel it, don't you? Oh please, if you can hear me, kill them."

128

When she raised her head, her lips were red.

Deep in forest, under the dappled light of a pale moon, the first of the men began to scream.

All Tales Must End

Michelle Muenzler

Michelle Muenzler, known at local science fiction and fantasy conventions as "The Cookie Lady", writes fiction both dark and strange to counterbalance the sweetness of her baking. Her short fiction and poetry can be read in numerous science fiction and fantasy magazines, and she takes immense joy in crinkling words like little foil puppets. For a dose of squidgy weirdness, check out her novella, "The Hills of Meat, the Forest of Bone", at Amazon. Just don't say she didn't warn you...

The city is dying. Children gather around my stall, half a plaza away from the cool shadows of the great cistern, and wait for tales. Their eyes are still bright despite the crust that grits their lids and the red dusty smears that stain where they last wiped the hollows of their cheeks. The line at the cistern snakes through the plaza, but its winding is more like a husk of skin than the snake itself. The people are deflated and drawn into themselves. But not the children. Not yet.

You would think life had always been like this, dust begetting more dust. Wind. Blue sky stretching into a purpled bruise horizon. The brittle salt-crust of the waste crackling beneath the city's sleep-curled claws. But every story has a beginning. And a middle. And yes, even an end.

I tell the children of when the city swam across the Great Waters and how the people wove nets of kelp and speared sharks with bone harpoons. I tell them of Kalessa who staked the first home atop the city's lacquered shell as it slumbered, her people's village crushed beneath its bulk.

I tell stories until dusk cools the air and the city lurches unsteadily to its feet and toward the first red glint of the Wayfarer's Star. By then, all the children are gone, gathered by parents done with bargaining for every drop of water, or simply wandering off on their own in search of lizards and hidden treasure.

I dismantle the small cloth frame that names me storyteller and shields me during the worst heat of the day. My cup is empty of coins, but money means little to me now.

The city is dying.

There's a tremble to its step, an uncertain tremor. Death shudders beneath its gargantuan feet and shivers in its bones. Everyone knows it. I can see it in their clouded marble eyes as they skirt each other warily in the market. Yes, the city is dying, and with it, us. Who can value a copper against that?

**

A coin falls into my cup.

"Tell me," says a young man. "Of Kalessa's first year atop the city." His lips are generous, though chapped and broken; his eyes are spare and gray. "Tell me of how she prostituted herself to the Wayfarer so he'd set a star for the city to follow and never crush another village beneath its feet. Tell me of the first family she tricked into the city by inviting them to stay the day and poisoning them with a month of sleep."

I shake the cup, let the coin scrape against the clay and break the sonorous rhythm of his voice. "It sounds as though you already know those stories well enough."

"Then tell me of the week it rained fire and ash. Tell me who lived and who died and who slipped away in the night never to be seen again."

The three children seated before me gaze in rapt attention at the young man.

I flip the coin to his feet. "Those are not the stories I tell."

"No," he says. "But they should be."

He turns and walks a dozen steps away, then pulls a cloth frame from his back and sets up his own storyteller's booth. One of my girls wavers, her eyes darting between the two of us. Then she snatches the fallen coin and scurries to the young man's booth where she settles in and drops the coin into his cup. He begins his story, but I shut out the words and focus on my remaining listeners.

There have been rivals before, but in the end, the children always return to me.

***

I am breaking my fast with a bit of stale bread along the low wall of the tail rim when the young man finds me again. The broken salt-crust of the waste flashes beneath the rising sun.

"The Watchers have spotted a city," he says, shielding his eyes.

"I know."

"Then shouldn't you be at the head with the others looking for its shadow on the horizon?"

I finish my bread and wipe the crumbs from my lips. "It will come whether I see it or not."

He nods as though I have said some great sage thing. A flush sparks unwilling in my cheeks; I do not want to please him.

"Besides, it is too crowded to see anything right now. I'll go later."

He laughs, a low rumble that chills the warmth from my bones. "Your stories will do well today, I think. But tomorrow will be mine."

"Tomorrow belongs to the Wayfarer alone."

I can feel his gaze on me, but I keep my eyes upon the rising sun and the glittering path leading from it to the tail of our city. He pulls away from the wall and the edge of my vision.

"Tomorrow," he says, the laughter gone from his voice.

By the lack of alternating chill and heat, I know then he is gone, but an uneasy splinter has lodged itself in my breast. He knows something I do not.

Perhaps the Wayfarer has spoken in his dreams.

***

The young man is right. Several coins find their way into my cup that day, and my booth is crowded with children begging for my tales. Even a few adults stop by and listen, swaying slightly beneath the sun with a faint smile on their lips. Some share their water with me when my voice turns dry.

I speak today of ancient encounters with foreign cities, of Jorubar and the Snakes of Imm, of Danyel who fought off a thousand soldiers of the Three-Fold Emperor in the hour before sunset. In the end of all the stories, our city rises to the Wayfarer's Star and moves on.

Twice, I break down my booth and visit the head wall, but I cannot push my way through the crowds, and they do not part for me. I hear broken words humming from their lips, though:

The city will be great. The city will be poor. They will have water. They will take what water we have left. We are staying. We are going.

At dusk, I slide instead through the lesser crowds of the right rim and strain to see the new city. It is far. Too far to know anything until tomorrow. It stands as a dark shadow swallowed by the red of the setting sun. Several families have already gathered at the lifts, shuffling for the best spot in the morning and holding their children close against the night. Their lives are compressed in tight packets upon their backs.

I cannot sleep. Half the night, I watch the Wayfarer's Star and pray for our city to be saved. The other half, I wonder if perhaps it is time for even me to leave. I can count the years in the stories and know how long our city has lived, but nothing tells me how long it takes for a city to die.

I suppose the true answer is they are the same.

***

When sleep catches me at last, it drowns me. Voices clamber atop one another in my dreams, struggling to be heard, and above us all, the Wayfarer's Star watches. When I wake, dawn is well past and the Wayfarer's Star is gone. The cistern line shuffles like the dead, and whispers crawl through the dust.

Only one voice is bright and clear--the young man's. His booth is open and filled with shadow-eyed adults. The children are held tight against their parents' breasts, or strangers' where no parents are to be found. Their eyes are dull as stones.

The young man is telling of Izura who built a boat to take the people from the city when it seemed the Great Waters would never end. In my stories, he is Izura the Traitor for the children he lured onboard and stole away. The young man calls him Izura the Brave.

There is something wrong with the city we have found. I do not have to see it to know this. But my curiosity must wait. I pull out my cloth frame and raise it beneath the sun.

The young man has started a war, and I will not lose.

***

When the day is finished, I can count on both hands the number of people who stopped at my booth, and most simply shook their heads and slid into the young man's crowd. There were no children at all. I slip away from the market as the setting sun paints everything a violent shade of red. The right rim is abandoned. Even the houses bolted on the shell's slant have their shutters closed tight.

And now I see why.

The city we have found is dead. We will leave it behind us tonight, but I can see it clearly now, several shell-lengths away. Crumbling spires reach for the sky, their faded tops winking with the promised glint of gold. The walls are red, like the waste, and gleam from the salt-dust encrusted on their remains.

Yet all of this would not be enough to justify the emptiness snaking through my chest. I have seen dead cities before.

But the city also lies atop the half-buried wind-scoured remains of a great beast like our own. A bleached green, far quieter than the one beneath my feet, peeks between the buildings and bones. The remnants of a shell.

I cannot stop the tears that wash down my cheeks. A waste of water in these dry times. If I could gather my tears, I would have drink enough for a lifetime. When the sun falls beneath the horizon and our city rises, I turn away from the carcass of the other and dry my eyes.

How many cities like our own have died in this waste? And how many more are buried in our path?

***

The next morning, the young man's lips smile as he raises up his stall, but his eyes are hollow. A crowd gathers early for his tales, their backs turned to me. They belong to him now. I can picture collars buckled around their throats with leashes leading to the young man's swaying hands. He begins the story of Haiden the Mad who tossed those he deemed unworthy from the head of the shell so they might be trampled beneath the city's feet. He calls him Haiden the Just.

I can listen no more. This plaza no longer feels like home. There are no children to be seen. I wander to the tail of the sleeping city and watch the sun pass over our wake.

***

"You can still change your stories," the young man says three days later. "It is not too late."

We are like the moon and tide, he and I. Wherever I go for peace, he finds me, yet something unwilling colors his eyes when we meet. And how could I have thought them to be just gray? They are every color of the rainbow in the dawn light. I could watch them forever, but close my own instead. Fine grains of dust blow across my closed lids and cling to my lips.

"You twist your stories," I say.

"And you do not?"

He is so close, I can hear him breathing. He sounds like the wind.

"There is no truth in stories," he says. "You know that. Just the lies handed from one generation to the next."

"If you don't believe, then why tell them at all?"

His silence lingers over the both of us, but I know he is not gone. Not yet. The tide knows when the moon is near. If he will not answer one question, though, then I will ask another.

"What is your name?" I should have asked a week ago. There is too much power in the unnamed.

I feel him pulling away from me, and I blindly reach out and grasp his arm.

"You should tell my stories," he says, his voice behind me now. He gently pulls his arm free, and when next I open my eyes, he is gone.

***

Three more days, and three more corpses of great cities, all buried beneath the weight of tumbling buildings on their backs. The third night, our city stumbles and falls to its knees. One home breaks loose and plummets to the waste below, taking a family of eight with it. I did not see it happen, but I heard the crack of its foundation in my dreams. I felt the children screaming.

In the morning, I do not set up my storyteller's booth, but watch the young man instead. The crowd around him today is all men. Who else could listen to his stories after such tragedy? Sometimes I find his gaze skirting across my own. His words are aimed at me, but I no longer hear them. As dusk gathers, he leaves his crowd. The men nod their heads to him and to each other as he passes, then leave in small groups. I try to sleep, but the city's steps, once comforting, now fill me with dread. Eventually, I rise and walk the streets, looking to the night sky for relief. As I near the tail wall, the city takes another step, and the sound of crunching stone joins the usual shudder. My heart stops, and I wait for the screams. Something crashes far below the city. It is quiet then except for a low scraping, the sound of stone grating against shell...and the voices of men.

I pad down the street, down the shell, down to where the voices are stronger. Down to the tail wall where everything is wrong. Where the wall once stood is now a gaping hole. Rubble is gathered along its edges. There are men at the wall and elsewhere, men whose faces I know from the market today. But I do not want to recognize their faces now. They are covered in dust, the pale gray dust of our homes, not the red of the waste. Several of them are pulling at the bolts holding down one of the tail rim homes. The bolts clatter and roll one by one through the wall breach. Other men are pushing an already freed home down the shell. Before long, the shell's slant takes over and the home screeches through the wall breach, leaving deep scores through the shell where it passed. I hear a shattering below. But no screams. Nothing but the murmurs of men and popping of bolts and low thud of the city's feet.

I cannot understand why nobody has come out, why I am alone. Somebody must stop this madness. I cling to the nearest house, slide around to the front door, and start to bang. The door falls open. It wasn't even fully closed. On the floor, bodies are piled atop one another, blood leaking from split skulls.

There is screaming now. It is my own, but I cannot stop it. I fall

139

to my knees and take a child's still-warm hand in my own. A shadow falls over me from behind. The moonlight is gone.

"You shouldn't have done that," says a man's voice, coarse from too much dust.

There is a whistle, and a wet thud reverberates through my skull. The child slips away, the floor slips away. Darkness slides into their place. And all I can wonder is if this is how my story ends. I had hoped for a better tale.

***

I am dead. I expected silence or the soft voice of the Wayfarer, but the darkness is filled with screams and the thud of flesh. My skull throbs.

I should be dead, but I am not.

A crust has sealed my eyes. I scrape it free, and then open my eyes to more darkness. Only this darkness is pricked by starlight. And the stars are sliding, slowly sliding. And there is scraping. And the door hangs open, and through it are great gouges in the city's shell.

It is not the stars that are sliding. It is the house.

I drag myself frantically through the door as the house grates another foot downward. Outside, men struggle against other men. Several are sprawled near me, their eyes open but blank. There will be no more stars for them.

It is when the house begins to slide unstopping that I remember the hand I clasped before the darkness took me. The hand of a child. I spin back toward the house, but the world spins with me, and I fall to my knees. The house slips downward, then over the edge and shatters far below. The child is gone. They are all gone.

Only madness remains.

I do not know who will win the battle around me. Nor do I care. I drag myself foot by foot up the shell and away from the melee. If I watch it, I will be forced to remember each blow. I will be asked what I saw and what I heard and what it all means. But I do not think there are any answers. If there are, I do not want to find them. And watching will change nothing.

All stories have a beginning. A middle. And an end. Always an end. I was taught this by my mother when she passed on her art to me.

The young man is the end of this story. This truth aches in my bones with every inch I gain toward safety. The screams die behind me. Everything dies behind me. Ahead, the Wayfarer's Star watches and leads us onward.

The young man's stories must be stopped.

***

The knife is easy to find. Every street corner vendor sells them this morning. Nobody wants to die undefended. Nobody wants to be left bleeding in the waste. I have no coppers, but I weave a tale of helplessness until a passerby takes pity and purchases a knife for me.

The young man said there is no truth in stories, but that is a lie. The truth is in the ending. Always in the ending.

***

Dusk scrapes its early fingers across the horizon. The young man finishes his last story and packs away his cloth frame. The crowd parts, each nodding their heads when he passes.

I follow him from the market. My knife is not well-made--the tang too shallow, the blade too thin--but it should do. I hope it will snap in his heart so that he cannot pull it free. I want to hear him scream. For the child last night who could not.

He slips quietly through the streets, nodding at strangers and making his way closer to the head of the city. Soon it is just him and I. All others are barring their doors and tightening their shutters.

At the head, he steps to the wall and spreads his fingers across the stones. I creep up, the setting sun watching over us both. Behind him, I raise my knife and draw a deep breath. His stories leave me no choice.

With a jerk, I plunge the blade into his back. It snaps, and I drop the handle to the ground and wait for him to fall.

But he does not.

"The end is not that easy," he says, turning to face me.

I was wrong about his eyes. They are neither gray nor rainbowed, but red. Like the wasteland sand. Like blood.

I cannot speak. My tongue is lost.

"This is not one of your market tales to be spun in endless circles. You think you own this story, but it does not belong to you. It belongs to those who gave it birth."

I shield my eyes against the setting sun, against him.

"It will all be over soon. Tomorrow. Enough has been done. This daughter will make it home." He turns back to the sun. "When the time comes, you will tell your people to go north. The waste ends. Eventually. Some might survive to see it."

"I don't--" My throat catches. "I don't understand."

The sun's last edges dip against the horizon.

"Tomorrow," he says.

The sun slips away, and the young man flashes into a cloud of dust. Wind scatters him down the street. I reach out and touch the wall where his hands were a moment ago. Nothing. Nothing but a lie of flesh.

In the purpled sky above, the Wayfarer's Star flares, and the city rises.

***

At dawn, the city does not stop. Nor does the Wayfarer's Star fade. People mill restlessly in the market. They ask strangers for answers and give their own when asked. But all of them are wrong.

My booth is open, but nobody stops.

"Go north," I say. "The end is near."

They shy away and seek their answers elsewhere. The young man was right, so many days ago. I have been telling the wrong stories, and now the people will not listen to me. A heaviness settles on my shoulders. I bow my head and stare at the heaving shell beneath me. My words are nothing now.

The thin voice of a child interrupts my despair.

"What's north?" she asks.

I look up. It is the girl who first went to the young man's booth. She has aged much in such a short time, but something strong still glints in the stones of her eyes.

She is silent, and I realize she is waiting for me to speak.

"North," I say. I had not thought beyond the warning. I have no stories of north to tell.

She stares, and the weight of her patience draws her shoulders downward until they can give no more. And still I cannot find a story. She turns to leave.

"Wait," I say, and dig deep into my bones. "North. North is the land of the chosen. It is the hidden valley the Wayfarer has dug into the earth for those who have guarded his children on their long journey. North is--"

She sits at my feet and smiles, and I continue my lies of sweet-water streams and hillsides clustered with grapes. More children gather as the day lengthens. Some of them leave eventually, and I tell them to spread the tale, to make it their own. We all must be storytellers today. They smile and nod and rejoin their restless families. And on all their lips is a single word: North.

At noon, we see the coming of the end.

The Watchers cry out first. "The end of the world! The end of the world!"

The people's screams are swallowed by the city's relentless footsteps.

"North," I say, one last time, and the children nod even as they scramble to their feet.

When the last one is gone, I take down my cloth frame and make my way to the right rim wall. Far ahead of the city is the end. It is not what I expected at all. A jagged edge of red rock glitters beneath the noon light, marking the world's edge, and then there is nothing but a star-filled void untouched by the sun. The Wayfarer's Star shines brighter than I have ever seen it. The city's step increases, and the buildings shudder at the pace.

The wall becomes crowded with families struggling to gain access to the lift. Some throw ropes over the side and clamber to the waste below. As the crowd at the wall grows, I force my way against them and go toward the head of the city, to the spot where I last saw the young man.

Across the waste, people scatter in the city's wake. Some north, some south, and some back to the endless east. I think more north than not, but I cannot be sure. There is nothing more for me to do, regardless.

The city is deserted by the end. I wait and watch as the last people turn to ants behind me, and then I turn my head back to the Wayfarer's Star. The moon and tide, I think. The young man is wrong. This is my story as much as anyone's. My beginning is here, and so shall be my end.

The edge of the world is three steps away. Now two. Now one. I pull in one last breath, heavy with dust.

And the city steps into the stars.

Hunting the Blue Rim

R. L. Martínez

R. L. Martinez writes SFF fiction with dark edges & corners. She lives in Norman, OK with her husband, two young children, a mouse-killing cat, & two naughty pooches.

Spur had hunted this vast swath of forest before. Known as the Blue Rim – from the Strays' enclaves it looked like a blue-green streak – it undulated its way to the far horizon. She licked her lips in anticipation and snapped her fingers to call out her witchlight. It pooled in her palm, casting a white-blue glare over the rocky hill on whose crest she now stood. The way down into the Blue Rim was perilous even at the best of times, but in the failing light of sunset, it could mean a painful death should she miss a step and tumble to the bottom. Genesis and the other elders said the Blue Rim had once been something called an "oshun", an enormous body of salty water in which strange animals fed and lived and slept. Spur loved stories about What Came Before, though she did not really believe them anymore; not since she left childhood behind when she began her monthly courses.

Her muscular legs and supple feet picked over the rocky hill with meticulous care, bare toes gripping the embedded chunks of twisted metal and stone she had to climb over and down. The stories held that these ruins were all that remained of a great city, destroyed by war centuries ago. Indeed, above the Rim lay a field littered with the detritus of What Came Before, now reclaimed by forest. At the bottom of the hill, she squatted and searched the ground. Her eyes lit when she saw the edge of a print set in a patch of mud. Rain had come several days ago, soaking the fields and refilling the Strays' wells. Here under the trees of the Blue Rim, the ground had not quite dried, thus capturing the mago's print. The size indicated a male of considerable proportions. She crept closer. He must have come here in search of more ruins. The Blue Rim was a holy place for many, including the Strays and the people of Modoa. Indeed, the magos often came on pilgrimages to pray at the shrine of the Green Lady, who lay further on. That was when the hunts began. The Strays felt the magos move through the Blue Rim. The subtle lines of power embedded in the ground trembled and sent vibrations back to the Strays' elders. And so a hunter was sent. This time, it was Spur's turn.

The sun had truly set now and the forest stretched out its shadows in ever-deepening pools. Spur could go on, continue to track, but hunger and weariness – it was a five day walk from her home to the Blue Rim, after all – would mean she might face her prey at less than optimal condition. That would not do. She had only one chance left now and had to use every advantage she had to ensure success.

Besides the plentiful plants that provided food, the forest was alive with game. Rabbit, deer, goat, ground fowl, even a vicious cow sometimes made an appearance. And, of course, the unicorns. But the likelihood of the Green Lady blessing her to that degree seemed impossible. Not with two failed hunts behind her.

Other predators roamed here too. Giant cats with fangs and claws like knives, wild dogs, snakes so big they could devour an adult whole. And then there were the Unwholesome. Those creatures who appeared near the end of What Came Before and operated outside the laws of nature. Most of them were extinct now, wiped out by the Modoan magos and the Strays. But a few remained and they were terrible to meet.

As Spur walked in the general direction of the Green Lady, she picked edible berries and fruits in case she could not bring down a meat source. But then she saw a print quite different from the first one she had seen near the bottom of the rise. It was a cloven hoof, small. A spark of excitement leapt to life beneath her breast bone. Spur removed her bow from her back. Her staff went into its loop on her leather back plate, across the quiver of arrows. That was not for hunting food, even if she were hunting unicorn. Her staff was only to be used in the bringing down of a mago. She set her collection of vegetation on the ground and pushed dead leaves and loose dirt over it to discourage all but the most determined of foragers. More hoof prints led the way and she took out an arrow, nocking it to her tightly strung bow. She extinguished her light. Later, it might be useful to blind and confuse her prey, but for now she must use only her senses of touch, taste, and smell to find her way.

Spur placed each step carefully, feeling for impediments that would either cut her bare feet or give away her location. Ahead, starlight lit up a small clearing. She could not see prints in the darkness but she smelled the distinct tang of animal dung. This she followed to the clearing. And there, bathed in dim luminescence while it munched on the sweet grass of the meadow, was a unicorn.

Tears filled Spur's eyes. Never in her short life had she dared hope to see an actual unicorn. The Strays' dwellings were covered in paintings of the holy beasts; clay fetishes stood on every windowsill; the robes of the priestesses were embroidered with their likeness; and a very few – those born with the sign of the Green Lady on their bodies – bore tattoos of unicorns. But to see one in the flesh was the secret dream of every Stray. It stood, no larger than an outsized wolf, like a blue star on four spindly legs much like a deer's and its body was spare and light like a deer's too. Its long tail, tipped in a brush of cobalt hair, curled and whipped around its flanks. Blue fur sprouted over its leg joints and chin. A graceful neck arched from its shoulders topped by a head something between a goat's and a deer's, delicate and sweet. But betraying its true nature were sharp incisors reaching from below its upper lip and the spear of white bone sprouting from the middle of its brow. Beauty and death in one perfect animal, the embodiment of the wild world and the Green Lady's most holy and rare envoy in the world. Spur did not want to kill it. It was too beautiful. It seemed the height of sacrilege. But to refuse such a gift would offend the Green Lady, perhaps curse her entire hunt. "To see a unicorn was a blessing," the Strays' elders said. "To kill one during a hunt a mark of favor. To feast on one, a source of power." Spur mouthed a prayer of thanksgiving to the Green Lady and raised her bow. The wood creaked slightly but that was enough to rouse the unicorn's attention. It raised its dainty head and bared its teeth in warning. "Lady, guide my arrow," Spur whispered and let loose her shot as the unicorn bunched its muscles to spring at her. The arrow, indeed, flew true and planted its barbed head in the beast's breast. The unicorn gave a melodic cry – lovely even in death – and stumbled to the ground. It gave a last shuddering breath and then went still. A clean kill.

Spur stood dumbly, unsure what to say or do. No one she knew had ever killed a unicorn. She had not even known before this moment if it was possible to wound one with mortal weapons, despite what the elders said. Perhaps it was *not* dead after all. Perhaps it would spring up and ram its lovely horn into her chest, or bite out her throat with its teeth. Spur approached, cautiously drawing the hunting knife from the sheath strapped to her thigh. She held it ready as she knelt beside the gleaming creature and laid a hand on its still-warm side. Her fingers were black against the sapphire-blue pelt. Her held-back tears dripped down her face. "Forgive me, beauty. I thank you for the sacrifice. I thank the Green Lady for this gift. May I walk in worthiness from this night on." She kissed each of its hooves. Then, hesitating for only a few blinks, she split the unicorn's belly, spilling out its entrails. She put down her knife and swam her fingers through the fragrant warmth of its innards until she found the plum-sized heart. With a great jerk, she pulled it free and held it up. Blood ran down her arm. Its redness surprised her. She had half-expected, in the ignorant way of the young, for the blood to be silver or gold, or even clear as water. It both disappointed and comforted her to see that even a legend bled the same as any other animal. Spur held up the heart. "For the glory of the Strays and the Green Lady." Blood jetted across her tongue as she bit into the warm organ. Much of it was tough, but she ate it all anyway. Next was the liver, a little larger than the heart, but softer and easier to chew.

She left the rest of the carcass for the predators who stalked the Blue Rim, a gift to thank them for leaving her in peace. The Strays did not take trophies, especially not from animals considered sacred. Hunting was not a sport or game. Since she was not in a position to make use of the hide and bones – as she would if hunting near her enclave – she left them for the forest and the Green Lady to reclaim and remake.

She cleaned her bloodied hands and knife on the grass, replaced the blade in its sheath, then returned to her cache of fruit. As she put distance between herself and the unicorn's carcass, she munched her tiny harvest. Finding a resting place in a fallen tree, hollowed out by time and insects, she curled up in its fragrant belly and slept.

The next day, she reached the Green Lady herself.

This clearing was much bigger than the one in which she killed the unicorn. The trees had made valiant attempts to crowd against the crumbling stone and mangled metal slicing up from the ground around the hill that rose from the center of the clearing, but had yet to overtake it. Spur, pausing her search for more of the mago's prints, struggled up the steep incline until she stood beside the enormous star-shaped plinth and looked into the face of her goddess.

Only fragments remained of what the elders said had been a mighty monument during What Came Before. The crook of an enormous elbow holding a tablet with raised letters etched on it. Most of the writing was indecipherable to her, but Spur could make out one word. She stopped now and gazed with shining eyes at her goddess' message to the world. "JULY IV MDCCLXXVI", she whispered. She did not understand what it meant, but "July", she knew, meant the same as "Julio", the name of the Strays' most holy month. She shivered as though she had spoken one of the sacred incantations used during a moon ritual.

Further off was the goddess' cracked face, lying half buried in the ground. Spur had been here twice before to ask the Green Lady's blessing during each of her failed hunts. The goddess had not seen fit then to grant her success. Indeed, Spur had suffered physical injury and unutterable humiliation. The memory of it made her chest tighten, her palms grow damp. This was her last chance. She approached the ruined visage and fell to her knees. The Green Lady's sad eye and mouth, the only features to have survived, seemed to invite Spur to sit and talk, pour out her worries.

"I'm afraid I will fail again. I don't want to see the shame and disappointment on the faces of my kin should I return to them for a third time. I don't want my magic to die." She bowed her head as tears slipped from her eyes. "Please, help me. I won't go home again. I will win the mago or disappear into the Blue Rim and let it finish me as it chooses." Spur clenched her hands into fists. At eighteen she had attempted this same hunt, though the quarry had been different. For a full month she had searched until she had had no choice but to admit that the vibrations of her prey had long since wavered and disappeared. She had returned home, having never even set eyes upon the mago. For two years, she endured the pity and disappointment of her clan while she trained relentlessly for another attempt. On her twentieth name-day, she had struck out again. This time, she cornered her quarry, a female, in a ravine overgrown with suckling vine. They had fought for hours, but the other woman had won and walked away, leaving Spur wounded and shamed. The disgrace had been even worse when she returned to her clan a second time.

No, she would not go home unmarked again. She refused to spend her life in perpetual childhood and servitude while her magic remained asleep and caged until it shriveled and died inside her. But the Green Lady had sent a unicorn – and that changed everything. Giving the goddess a final bow, she stood and searched around the ruins for signs of her prey. A breathy, joyous laugh leapt from her lips when she spied prints that matched the one she had found last night. They circled the plinth, stopped a ways away from the Green Lady – he had not come close for some reason – before doubling back and descending down the hill to the north. Spur turned back to the Green Lady and bowed deeply. "Thank you."

As she made her careful way down the hill, she saw movement in the trees ringing the clearing. On instinct, she froze and hefted her staff. Magic vibrated up her legs, making her entire body shiver. Her own power struggled to awaken, to respond to the energy calling to it. *He's here.* Spur licked her lips and continued down the hill, eyes fixed on the trees.

Fingers slippery on the wooden shaft of her staff, she approached the shade of the trees. Excitement and fear rushed through her veins. She had to consciously calm her breathing lest it give her away. Ducking beneath low-hanging branches, she entered the shadow of forest. A hedge of nettles blocked her way. She blinked at the living wall, at first uncertain if she was dreaming. Turning her head, she looked to either side and saw the hedge ran in each direction until it left her sight. This was no natural growth. The mago had put it there to stop her. As if to confirm her suspicion, she heard a deep chuckle on the other side of the nettles. "Go home, little witch. You're outmatched. Go home and serve your priestesses, look after the children of your clanswomen. Go home where it's safe." Spur's breath snagged in surprise. Not only did the mago speak the Strays' language without accent or hesitation, as if it was his mother-tongue, but it was the same dialect as Spur's enclave. Had he come from her home? Perhaps she even knew him, knew his family.

"Nothing to say, witch? I thought not. I'll be on my way, then. Safe journey back to your shack and dirt-patch of an enclave."

Spur ground her teeth against his scorn. Her hands ached as she gripped her staff until it creaked. "I have the blessing of the Green Lady! She has given me with the power of one of her unicorns."

A long pause followed her shouted rebuttals. Spur almost hoped he would dissolve the wall between them and surrender. Almost. But a mago who yielded so easily was not worth having. At last, in a voice now quiet and free of mockery, he said, "Then use it, little witch." The vibration of his magic lessened as he moved off.

Spur clenched her teeth and surveyed the thorny obstacle again. She could try to find its end, but it might take days, depending on whether the mago did not keep adding to it the closer she came to bypassing it. Meanwhile, he would reach the outer edge of the Blue Rim and be beyond her reach.

Spur touched one of the thorns, it was half the length of her thumb and wickedly sharp. Her own magic could not circumvent such a spell. Until she claimed her teacher and opened her power completely, she was left with nothing but calling forth witch-light and other tiny spells, amusing and often helpful, but without any true power to change things. "Magic takes both talent and will; power and blood." Those were Genesis' parting words to her six days ago. The hunt was as much a test of a witch's endurance as it was a pursuit of her magical awakening.

Closing her eyes, Spur brought the head of her staff to her lips. The large, unpolished agate embedded in the wood gleamed faintly. "Show me the way." She lowered the staff again towards the nettles. With a groan, Spur thrust it into the hedge and cleared an opening just large enough for her to enter. Immediately, she was enclosed in a suffocating half-light. Thorns hooked in her skin, tore at her shift. Panic, like a cold, iron spike in her chest, threatened to steal her courage. But she kept her eyes closed, one arm raised before them to keep the thorns from plucking them out, and followed the tug her staff. The agate hummed as it picked up the faint trace of the mago's power. It pulled her, like a magnet, in the right direction. Spur held on, though blood soon made the wood slippery. Thorns dragged at her cropped hair, jerking tufts of it free from her scalp. Blood trickled from hundreds of places up and down her body. Hours seemed to pass before she fell from the nettle wall and landed in a bleeding, whimpering heap on the other side. For several minutes she lay gasping against the pain, unable to bear the thought of inspecting her wounds. But, she finally pushed up from the ground and cast a fearful gaze over her body. Her shift hung from her shoulders in blood-smeared ribbons. Her dark skin had not fared much better. Releasing her grip on the staff, she struggled out of her back plate, emitting small yelps of pain as it slid over the cuts and nicks covering her arms. The ruined shift came off next. Only her back, protected by the thick leather of the plate had escaped unscathed. Her shift had protected her from the worst of the thorns, but, even so, she bore shallows cuts along her ribs, chest, buttocks, and thighs. Her limbs and face had endured the majority of damage. She needed to wash and treat the wounds, but that would have to wait as, through the haze of pain, the thrum of the mago's magic called her.

Anger, bright and hot, rose like a cleansing flood, washing away the worst of her pain. Spur struggled to her feet. Wincing and biting her lips so she would not shout, she heaved the back plate on again and picked up her staff. Now nearly naked, she followed the pulse of magic. Behind her bloody footprints marked her path.

As darkness once more overtook the Blue Rim, Spur called up her witch-light and cast its glow over the trees and bushes. The blue-white flame marked the places the mago's scent and magic spotted the ground and underbrush. No switchbacks that she could see, only a straight path through the woods. She doubted this lack of opposition meant he was ready to surrender. His kind did not capitulate easily, if at all. And Spur would not want it any other way. After two humiliating disappointments she wanted nothing less than complete triumph. And there was her rage to satisfy now. She *wanted* a fight. She wanted to pay him in kind for the blood she had spilled today.

Soon, wood-smoke, mingled with the sharp scent of water on stone, wafted to her on the evening air. She extinguished her witch-light and allowed her nose to lead her. Full dark had fallen by the time she stepped from the night-black forest and stood on the bank of a meandering river. Spur clutched her staff, lowering its head until it was leveled at her prey.

He crouched before a large fire, naked to the waist. Even bent over, she could see the Green Lady had made him large and fine. Here was a man who took pleasure in the physical as well as mental demands of life. Spur could have put his age anywhere between thirty and fifty. Magos knew how to stretch the years, make their bodies last for centuries or more. His trek through the Blue Rim had made him as dirty and unkempt as she. Cropped brown hair stood up in messy spikes. She could not see his face, but she imagined his beard and mustache better resembled the hedge of nettles than the neat symbols of power most male magos sported. The skin of his back, lighter than her own by only a shade or two, was crowded with tattooed spells. Her eyes roved over those swirling patterns hungrily. The sheer number of them coupled with their complexity spoke of battles fought and won. Soon, she would begin her own collection of spells, but only if she could convince this man to take her on as his apprentice. Head bent towards the fire, he turned a spit loaded with three fat rabbits. Too much for one person – even someone of his size. He had known she would come.

Though nearly imperceptible, her practiced eyes saw his entire body tense. "You're strong, little witch, I'll give you that."

Spur squared her shoulders and came closer as he rose and faced her. The fire behind him cast his face in shadow, but as she drew close, it became clearer. He did indeed sport a tangled beard, the same motley brown of his hair. His lips within that nest were thin and firm. He was not handsome by any means, too hard and spare for such a descriptor. But his eyes, those were the true attraction. They swirled with veins of green and blue and orange. They were eyes of power and wisdom. This man had

157

seen the Green Lady's true face – not just the shattered idol lying in the forest of the Blue Rim – but the eternal face of the universe. He had looked into the deep well of time and seen What Came Before.

She shrugged out of her back plate, just managing to suppress an agonized moan, and took a preparatory stance, staff ready across her body. "Do you surrender, mago?"

He emitted a sharp bark of laughter and crossed his arms over his inked chest. "To a little girl? You've done nothing but tax my patience, witch. I grew bored of your pitiful attempts to track me, so decided to enjoy a decent meal and rest."

Spur ground her teeth until the muscles in her jaw burned. But the pain helped her tamp down the fire of her anger. Genesis' voice creaked through her mind, *He'll say and do anything to rile you, make you lose control. Don't give in.* Spur's youthful temper had been her downfall during her second hunt. When her quarry had hurled insults at her, Spur had gone blind with rage, forgetting her training.

His smile widened. "If you don't like what I have to say. Either leave or shut me up."

Spur's eyes narrowed. *He's an empath.* He read her emotions too easily for mere insightfulness. She schooled her heart into a block of stone. She would give him nothing of her to feel – not until she had him in her net. "Do you surrender?"

Though his smile remained, it grew more thoughtful. "You want me, little girl? Come take me, if you can."

Spur curled her lips into a vicious grin and ground her toes into the dirt, using them to launch her at the mago. As she had expected, he feinted to the side and sent a bolt of power sizzling

158

towards her. She planted her staff against the ground and used it and the momentum she had built up to vault into the sky, above the paralyzing shot. She landed right in front of her quarry and swung her staff in a half-circle sweeping his legs out from under him. She had the satisfaction to see a brief look of surprised admiration on his face before he back-flipped over the fire. He landed in a warrior's crouch.

"No more smile, mago?"

"There's no one to tend you out here, little witch," he replied with a sneer. "When I thrash you, you'll be recovering for a week before you're able to limp back to your pathetic enclave."

Spur snarled. "Do you surrender?"

"To what? A bumpkin with a walking stick?"

Spur slammed the butt of her staff to the ground and blew into the fire. It snapped out towards the mago with a hungry roar. A pitiful little trick, but one that proved useful as he fell back and she leapt over the spit to pin him. He eluded her, though, rolling away and springing to his feet. He delivered a kick to her abdomen, throwing her towards the beach. Her staff flew from her hand and clattered against the rocks as the air rushed from her lungs in a painful whoosh. For a panicked moment, Spur could not breathe and her eyes bulged. From the corner of her vision, she saw the mago hurry towards her. He swung a bare foot through the air in another brutal kick. Spur grabbed a fistful of sand and grit, flinging it into his face. While he stumbled back, momentarily blinded, she lunged for her staff and brought it hard against his ribs. She felt something give with a sharp snick. The mago grunted and fell to one knee, right hand clutching his side. His breath rasped in and out in sharp pants. Spur leveled her staff at his throat. "Do you surrender?" Her voice was harsh and wheezy.

His laugh held no mockery now. "I can do this all night, little witch." His free hand shot out. With a soft cry, Spur watched her staff fly from her grip and into his waiting fingers. And before she could blink, let alone retaliate, he had cracked the wooden pole against her left arm, breaking the bone. She fell against the rocky beach again, bruising her already battered legs. He stood over her, staff held at the ready. "Do *you* surrender, witch?"

Spur clenched her teeth together and grabbed the wooden pole, palm over the agate. In her last gambit, she shoved all the power she had access to up the shaft. It ignited like a giant match and the mago let it go with an angry cry. Spur threw aside the flaming staff and struggled to her feet. On her way up, she grabbed a rock small enough to fit in her palm. Her left arm hung useless by her side but she saw the slight curl of the mago's body around the ribs she had smacked. Apparently, she *had* broken something. A satisfied smile curled one side of her mouth.

"Something amuses you, witch?"

She nodded. "This." She tossed the rock at him. For half a moment, his attention was divided and Spur took advantage of his distraction by launching her entire body into him. Pain like red lightning sizzled up her broken arm and radiated through her body as she made contact and sent him sprawling to the ground. She clutched him around the neck to control and guide their fall, making sure she landed on top. Her thighs gripped his torso and she pressed her right forearm against his throat. He stared up at her, their panting breaths mingling. Spur blinked against the nausea threatening to make her either vomit or faint. "Do... Do you surrender, m... mago?" She increased the pressure on his

160

neck when she felt his hands, pinned beneath her calves, ball into fists. Then, he suddenly went limp.

"Well fought, witch. I surrender."

Surprise made her gasp and let out the breath in a rush. She eased off his throat and sat up. "Truly?"

He laughed, though the sound was weak. "Yes, now get off me. You're heavier than you look."

Spur slid to one side and fought to stay conscious as her arm shrieked. He gasped sharply as he rolled to a kneeling position, one hand pressed to his ribs. With a grimace, he took hold of her left arm. Agony lanced up her shoulder and Spur tried to pull away. "Be still," he snapped. Soon, a steady warmth flowed up and down her arm, wrapping around the broken bone and knitting it back together. "Better?"

Spur nodded, relief causing tears to fill her eyes. He nodded sharply and released her. "Your first lesson begins now. Heal the damage you've done to me." He raised his right arm, exposing the ribs she had broken with her staff.

Eying him uneasily, Spur got to her feet and came to place her hands on his side. The elders taught the young ones about healing, whether they had magic or not. But until a witch's magic was opened, magical healings were something known only in theory. Still, Spur drew up those long-ago lessons in her mind, picturing the drawings of the human body she had studied. She imagined the smooth curve of the ribs and softly traced her hands over his side over and over, willing the broken ends she sensed beneath the skin to move back together. He hissed, face contorted in an agonized grimace, but did not stop her or jerk away. Soon, his skin grew heated and Spur's palms tingled. And then she felt it:

something within her cracked open. She moaned at the pleasure-pain and closed her eyes. Power flooded down her arms and into the flesh beneath her hands. A deep groan preceded him lowering his arm and pushing at her hands. "Good. A little longer than I'd like, but speed will come with practice." He pressed the heel of his palm to his side. "You're thorough and clean at least." His goddess-touched eyes were shadowed as he stared at her and his mouth was pulled into a thoughtful frown. His fingers brushed her shoulder where a particularly deep cut from the nettle hedge still oozed blood. "That will teach me to underestimate the Stray women."

Spur chuckled tiredly. "I take it you're no longer bored?"

He dropped his hand and his frown softened. Not quite a smile, but it made him look less forbidding. "I have a feeling I'm going to have a lot of trouble with you, little witch."

"The Strays have a saying: 'Trouble makes the best teacher.'"

He smiled at last, a genuine smile, free of disdain. "So it is. I'm Nedo Maatias."

Spur raised her brows at the strange name. It was not Stray at all. His eyes narrowed a bit, as if daring her to question him. She pursed her lips instead. Time enough to find out the truth. "Spur."

"Well, Spur, now that you're under my protection as well as command, I command you to go and wash so we can treat your wounds. A sickly apprentice is no good to me. And we've a hard journey to make tomorrow."

Spur's grin unfurled across her face. "Yes, Master Nedo." She almost skipped to the edge of the water. Relief and joy made the pain from her cuts fade into a dull and bearable ache. Tomorrow they would go on to Modoa, the mago's city that lay beyond the

162

Blue Rim, and her training would begin in earnest. Someday, she would return to her enclave, burdened with gifts and stories for her clan. Genesis probably already knew about the success of her student's hunt. The vibration of Spur's newly awakened power would have traveled back to the old woman and the other elders through the miles of ground between her and them. She hoped they could also feel her happiness and gratitude.

As she stepped into the cool waves, she glanced across the shore and her heart tripped. There on the far bank, watching her with eyes like black crystal, stood a unicorn. It was larger than the one she had killed in the clearing and a paler blue. It slowly dipped its head, as if nodding to her, before it turned and slipped back into the darkness of the forest. Spur swallowed and looked over her shoulder at Nedo. He once more crouched by the fire with his back to the river this time, seemingly unaware of their visitor – though a wise apprentice never underestimated how much her master was aware of. Spur regarded the place where the unicorn had stood. "To see a unicorn is a blessing. To kill one during a hunt is a mark of favor. To feast on one, is a source of power." She licked her lips, hesitating over the finishing line of the proverb. "But to see one a second time, is a message from the Green Lady – a sign that she has her hand on your life." And mortals who attracted and held the Green Lady's attention rarely led peaceful lives, if one lent any credence to the elders' tales.

Master Nedo has no idea just how much trouble has stumbled into his life. Spur smiled at the adventure spreading out before her.

Thank You To Our Supporters

Many thanks to our patrons
and supporters, especially:

Cathrin Hagey

GriffinFire

Julia Patt

J'nae Spano

Lian Fournier

Maria Haskins

Martin Cohen

Natalie Weizenbaum

Tessa N

Tory Hoke

Want to see your name here? Become a patron!
patreon.com/lunastation

About the Cover Artist

Reiko Murakami, also known as Raqmo is a U.S. based concept artist and illustrator specialized in surreal fantasy and horror characters. Her work has been published in Spectrum, Infected by Art, ArtOrder Invitational: The Journal, Exposé, 2D Artist and many others.

You can find more of her work at:

www.reikomurakami.com

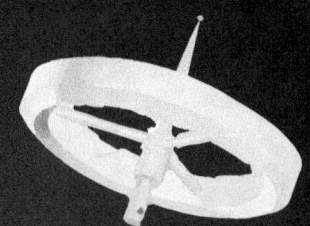

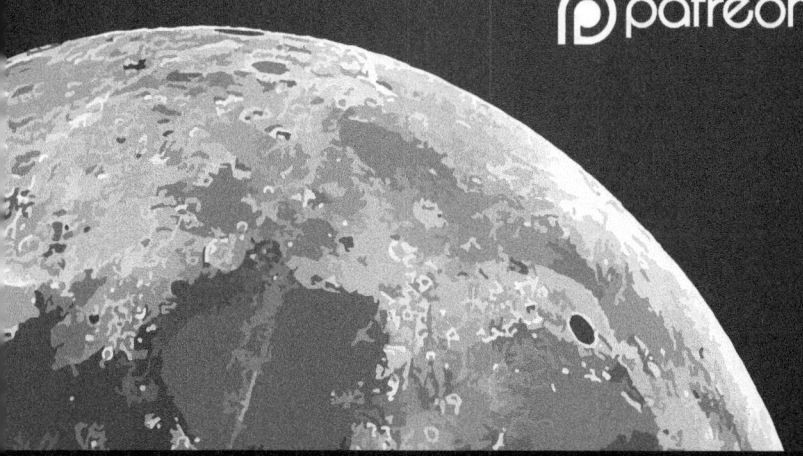

www.ingramcontent.com/pod-product-compliance
Lightning Source LLC
Chambersburg PA
CBHW071252130626
46556CB00003B/1276